CYNTHIA HICKEY

Cat-Eyed Witness
(A Tail-Waggin' Mystery)
By Cynthia Hickey

ISBN: 978-1-952661-45-7

DEDICATION

To cozy lovers everywhere!.

Chapter One

I unlocked the front door to Tail-Waggin' Love and glanced each way around the U-shaped strip mall. Mrs. Hedford, owner of Style Yourself, the local hair salon, gave a wave before entering her store. Mr. Mills, manager of the local hardware store, glared, then nodded before disappearing around the corner of the strip of small shops. In the center, Mrs. Parker swept the stoop of the drugstore. I loved the small-town feel of Waterfall, Arkansas, so much that I was part of a committee to keep big developments out, and I took my job very seriously.

"Good morning, Heather." I smiled at my best friend who worked part time in the pet daycare. "You're here early."

Heather tossed her dark hair over her shoulder. "Bobby doesn't have to leave for work for another hour or so and said he would drop the munchkin off at the babysitter's. After a night of crying and refusing to go to sleep, I needed the company of four-legged friends." Her toddler, Robby, was spoiled beyond belief but was such a cutie I didn't dare step in where I didn't belong. Besides, I loved the little tyke and could overlook the messes he made when circumstances caused Heather to bring him to work with her once in a while.

I held the door open for my regular morning visitors, Mr. Armstrong and his cuddly fat, tabby-cat, Moses. "Yay, coffee."

He laughed. "I hope my company is as pleasing as your morning java, Trinity Ashford."

"Most definitely." I took the offered drink and led him to a small table in the corner, then handed the one he'd brought for Heather to her. While he never forgot Heather, it was me he came to see.

Mr. Armstrong released Moses from his carrier, the cat immediately dashing off to find my cats, Trashcan and Sharkbait. He took his seat with a serious look on his face.

"Is something wrong?" I sat across from him and placed my hand over his wrinkled one.

"I'm getting some pressure to sell some of my property." He sat back. "Not only that, but someone wants me to divide these little shops into much larger ones and raise the rent."

My blood ran cold. I couldn't afford more rent. Not if I wanted to fulfill my dream of veterinary school. "What are you going to do?"

"Not sell, that's for sure." He smiled at me over the rim of his cardboard cup. "Don't worry your pretty little head, dear. I won't change our agreement. You watch Moses for a cut in rent and help ease an old man's loneliness. That's worth every cent."

"You're so good to me."

"You're the daughter I've always wanted and never had."

Warmth, more from emotion than the coffee, flooded through me, and tears pricked my eyes. Mr. Armstrong really was the kindest man I'd ever met. With my parents traveling Europe for over a year, he was the perfect stand in father. Not only did we share a love of God and animals, but we'd formed an unlikely friendship from the first day a year ago when he hired me to watch his furry darling.

"Who is pressuring you to subdivide?" I sipped the fragrant brew, closing my eyes in pleasure.

"Someone I haven't seen in a very long time." He waved a hand. "Let's not talk about unpleasant things. Tell me another of your engaging animal tales."

I regaled him with a story of two charming poodles I couldn't tell apart that had played games with me the day before. "Those two little guys had their strategy well planned out. I never knew whether I was dealing with Curly or Moe. I'd get one cornered after playtime only to find the other had escaped. It took me a while to realize there'd been two in Mrs. Rogers' carrier."

"You do have an interesting life, my dear."

Not really. Other than the pets in my care each day, I had no social life. Oh, sure, David, the UPS guy, kept asking me out on dates, and the library insisted I had a book out for the last two years, but other than that, I curled up each evening with my cats and a good book. It was enough.

"I have to rush this morning," he said. "A lot on my list today, but I wouldn't miss our morning coffee for anything." He stood, planted a kiss on my cheek, and tossed his cup in the garbage on the way out.

"You sure have that old man wrapped around your finger." Heather flipped the closed sign to open.

"He's a dear." I tossed my own half-finished drink in the garbage and prepared to start the day. Business was steadily climbing, and I could see my dream of becoming a veterinarian looming on the horizon.

Heather handed me the mail from the day before. "Another notice from the library."

I sighed. "I turned that book in. I know I did. Guess I'll have to pay for it and chalk it up as a loss."

"It can't be more than twenty dollars."

True, but I had that amount set aside for a new pair of sneakers. Plastering a smile on my face, I stepped behind the counter as the first customer of the day entered, sending the bell over the door jingling.

"Good morning, Mrs. Nelson." I fought to keep my smile in place. Regardless of the fact that Mrs. Nelson was the most difficult customer I had, she was a regular. Her poor schnauzer deserved all the fun she could get. "How is Greta this morning?"

"Cranky." She set the pet carrier on the counter. "Please don't let her out to play today. She came home so dirty yesterday it was quite an embarrassment for our dinner guests."

Dirty? I did my best to make sure the pets were returned as good, or better, than when dropped off. "We'll make sure that doesn't happen again." The poor dear. She couldn't be kept in a cage all day.

"I'll return for her at three. A lot to do." Mrs. Nelson wiggled her fingers at her dog, then hurried from the shop.

I peered into the carrier. "Oh, the tales you could tell if you could talk. What's that? You had pancakes for breakfast? You poor dear." The animal might not be able to speak, but the sweet smell of its breath and the remnants of syrup on her whiskers told the whole story. Why did some pet owners insist on feeding their animals people food?

When I fulfilled my dream of becoming a veterinarian, I would speak with each of my patients' owners and insist it be pet food only. "Come on, sweetie. Your home away from home is waiting for you."

Before I could enter the back of the shop, Trashcan, Sharkbait, and Moses raced past me, heading for the opening front door. I shoved the pet carrier into Heather's arms and rushed to herd the cats back before they escaped. The little minxes. I knew exactly what they were up to. If they heard the bell jangle over the door, they tried their escape routine every time. It was normally Heather's job to keep them corralled in the back. Hard to do while putting another animal away.

I grabbed Moses first, since he was often the ringleader, and dodged the man coming through the door. The cat hissed and fought his way out of my clutches, racing to the back of the room. I shook my head and sniffed. Ah, the visitor wore the cologne the cat didn't seem to like.

Danger averted, since my own cats followed their mischievous friend, I straightened to greet the stranger. "Welcome to Tail-Waggin' Love. I'm Trinity. May I help you?"

The handsome man glanced around the shop. "I was told Harvey Armstrong spent time here every morning. I was hoping to run into him."

"And you are?"

"Brad Armstrong, his son."

I froze on my way to the counter. "I wasn't aware he had a son."

"We've been …estranged the last few years." He smiled, revealing a dimple in his cheek. "But, it's all working out. I'm here to help him convert these old shops into something more modern."

So, he was the one who had Mr. Armstrong in a dither. "I'm sorry to hear that. You'll cause some people to be very unhappy." Including me. If my rent rose, attending school would be shoved further into the future, not to mention I would need to find another place to live. "Your father left a while ago. He said he had business to attend to." I stepped behind the counter. "Is there anything else I can help you with?"

"No." He gave me a smile that, despite my annoyance at his plan to ruin my life, sent my stomach flip-flopping. "Thank you. I'm sure we'll be seeing more of each other."

Watching him leave, I couldn't help but think that people like him were the reason I preferred the company of animals over humans. Animals didn't make plans to ruin a person's life.

"Who was that tall drink of deliciousness?" Heather closed the door to the kennels.

"He said he was Mr. Armstrong's son."

"You don't believe him?"

I shrugged. "I didn't ask for identification, but they did have the same eyes."

"You noticed his eyes? That's good. You aren't completely a hermit." Heather laughed.

My face heated. "Of course, I noticed. I'm not blind. You can stop any matchmaking attempts from taking root in your mind. He's here to run us out of business." I explained Brad's plan to subdivide the property. "There's no way I'll be able to afford the rent and save money."

Heather laid a hand on my arm. "It'll work out."

I lifted a shoulder. "I hope so. I do tend to worry needlessly sometimes."

"You're the worst." Heather smiled, taking some of the sting out of her words and grabbed cleaning supplies from under the counter. "I'll be washing the front window if you need me."

I might be needing a place to live, and Heather's large backyard in which to run my business if things progressed as Mr. Armstrong feared. I folded my arms and plopped my forehead against them. Every time I took a step forward in my goals, it seemed as if something happened to make me take two steps back. I sighed again. No sense feeling sorry for myself. I'd do my best to talk Brad out of subdividing the property I leased. Surely, the man could see reason when it was presented to him in a logical manner.

Heather knocked on the window to grab my attention, then pointed across the street. Mr. Tall, Dark, and Life Ruining was strolling back toward us.

Here was my next chance to talk him out of destroying everything I'd worked for.

Chapter 2

Brad waltzed through the door as if he owned the place, which in actuality, he probably did. I crossed my arms, prepared to do battle. With a smile on his handsome face, he approached the counter.

"Trinity. May I call you by your first name?"

I refused to be swayed by his charm or alluring aftershave. Instead, I'd focus on his plans and the fact that, to Moses, his cologne smelled anything but good. Animals were often a better judge of character than humans. I nodded. "Brad."

"Is there somewhere we can talk in private? I know you have a business to run, but this won't take but a few moments."

"We can sit at the table in the corner. My help will be leaving soon, and I can't go anywhere."

He nodded and motioned for me to go ahead of him. "This won't take long. I promise."

Of course, Heather decided the windows were clean enough and pretended to be busy at the counter. I ignored her and sat across from Brad.

Brad opened a briefcase and set a stack of legal-looking documents on the table. "I've been going over the company's rental agreements and have some concerns over your property."

My shoulders slumped. Things were moving way too quickly.

"You have one of the largest storefronts and pay the lowest rent." He narrowed his eyes. "Why is that?"

"I watch Mr. Armstrong's cat in exchange for partial rent." I sat on my hands to still their trembling.

"That still doesn't bring you to where you should be. You also live above the store." He leaned his arms on the table. "What exactly is your relationship with my father?"

I gasped. "Are you suggesting something improper?"

"Should I?"

"Absolutely not." It was a good thing my hands were under me, or I'd be going to jail for assault. "How dare you accuse me and that dear man of anything … other than friendship."

He raised his eyebrows. "I see. Well, I don't know my father as well as I once did, but I intend to remedy that. He has made some business decisions that aren't in the best interest of the company, and I'm here to make things right."

"By raising my rent?"

He nodded. "I'm sorry, but I don't see any other way. Now, about the apartment—"

"That's included in our agreement!" My world was tumbling around my feet. "But, Mr.

Armstrong—"

"—will see things my way in the end." He slid the papers back in his case and stood. "I will put a new lease agreement in the mail, effective three months from now when your lease expires." He pulled a business card from the breast pocket of his suit jacket. "Please call me if you have any questions."

Oh, I'd make a phone call all right. To his father. I remained seated, letting him show himself out and blinked back tears. "What are we going to do, Heather? This is awful."

"We need to increase our business." Heather worried her lip. "We'll take out an ad in the paper. Offer three-day pet boarding for the price of two. Maybe we should hire that groomer we've talked about."

"That all costs money."

"You have to spend money to make money. We need to draw in customers from the neighboring towns. I can understand why they wouldn't want to drive fifteen miles to use the pet care, but boarding is another story." Heather glanced at the clock. "I need to go. Pray about it. The answer will come. We have three months."

I buried my face in my hands. I had so much work to do, and now my mind spun like a child's windup toy. The phone rang, causing me to push aside my thoughts and get to work.

"Good afternoon. Tail-Waggin' Love. This is Trinity. How may I help you?"

"It's Mr. Armstrong." His normally friendly voice sounded curt. "Did you have a visit from my son?"

"Yes."

"I'll be right there." Click.

Now what? The last thing I wanted was to get in the middle of a father-and-son feud.

I headed to the kennels to let the dogs out, all except for poor Greta. The dog whined in greeting, spinning circles in her cage. "Sorry, girl. Mama's orders." I squatted, petting her through the wires. "Maybe tomorrow. No, I promise a bit of exercise this afternoon, you poor thing." I leaned my head against the door.

What advice would the animals give if they could talk? Who would care for them if I were forced to close my business? They'd be left home alone after being used to spending their day with playmates. I couldn't let that happen. They needed me.

"Trinity?"

I hurried to the front room where Mr. Armstrong gathered me in a hug. "Thank you for coming."

"Let's sit down." He led me to the table. "Tell me what Brad said."

"He's raising my rent in three months." I sniffed. "You know I can't afford that and go to school."

"Nothing is going to change for you, dear, not in a bad way. I told you that." A muscle ticked in his jaw, a jaw so similar to Brad's it took me back.

"But he has papers."

"I still have controlling shares in the company. Don't you trust me?" His eyes softened.

I nodded. "But, he seems so formidable."

"Only when he's working." He gave me a sad smile. "My son was once a very kind man. I told you my wife was killed, right? Yes, well, she was murdered during a home burglary. Brad has been driven ever since, as if working hard can erase the image in his mind of finding her on the kitchen floor. Instead of drawing us closer, it pushed us apart. I can handle my son. You take care of these lovely animals. It's what you were meant to do."

He always knew the right thing to say. "Thank you. I'll try not to worry anymore." I shook my head to push away my concerns.

"That's my girl." He grinned and stood. "I'll see you in the morning with coffee. Would you fetch my cat? I've decided to stay home today."

I rushed to do his bidding. What would I do without Mr. Armstrong? I'd felt so certain about the future I made the decision to pay for the lost library book right after work. It would be one less thing hanging over my head.

Chapter 3

Where was Mr. Armstrong? He hadn't missed morning coffee with me in three months, nor had he ever failed to leave his orange tabby, Moses, in my care for the day.

Nerves jumping like a cat on hot coals, I moved to boot up my computer. I might as well check emails while I waited. If he didn't show up in the next thirty minutes, I'd give him a call. There had to be a good reason for his absence. He wasn't the type to worry me without reason.

Exactly half an hour later with no response to my phone call, I hung a sign in the window of the pet care stating I'd be back soon. I locked the door and marched down the street toward the high-rise apartment building that overlooked the shabby but slowly improving Main Street of Waterfall, Arkansas.

The concierge, Mr. Appleton, greeted me with a

smile and ushered me inside the stylish building. "A fine morning, Miss Ashford."

"That it is, Mr. Appleton." If only I could rid myself of the nagging feeling that something terrible had befallen Mr. Armstrong, the cool autumn morning would be beautiful indeed. "Have you seen Mr. Armstrong this morning?"

"No, ma'am, he hasn't come down."

Taking a deep breath, I entered the elevator, pressed the button for the top floor, and took a tight grip of the polished wood bar encircling the death box. I kept my gaze locked on the numbers as the elevator rose, exhaling sharply when the doors opened on floor eighteen.

I took a few steps from the elevator and knocked on Mr. Armstrong's carved wooden door. When no answer came, I glanced around the small foyer. Was it possible he had an appointment he forgot to tell me about? I nibbled on my right pinkie nail. No, he had never failed to drop Moses off, not wanting the cat to spend one minute alone in the large penthouse. Something had to be wrong. I always prided myself on my gut instincts and didn't plan to stop now.

I knocked once more before reaching for the doorknob. It opened easily at my touch. Yes, something was definitely wrong. I sniffed. The fragrance of a strident cologne greeted me. It wasn't the brand Mr. Armstrong usually wore.

A cat's worried howl filled the air. "Moses? Here, kitty kitty." Usually a friendly animal, Moses hated one brand of cologne in particular. That could explain his caterwauling.

Instead of coming to my call, the howling increased, spurring me into the kitchen. When I caught no sight of the cat or his master—if cats could call a human their master—I headed for the living room.

Moses peeked from under the plush sofa, hissing at the sight of me. I bent over. "What's wrong, precious? You know me. We're buddies. You play with Trashcan and Sharkbait every day." My cats, who had the run of the pet day care, seemed to look forward to Moses's daily visits.

The cat hissed again and zoomed toward the bathroom. I straightened, then followed the frightened feline. I cornered him next to the vanity and scooped the animal into my arms.

He immediately settled down and began to purr. I nuzzled my face in his soft fur and stepped into the bedroom. And froze.

Mr. Armstrong lay fully dressed on the embroidered coverlet of his four poster bed. From his chest protruded a butcher knife. I gasped and dropped Moses, who immediately made a dash for the bathroom again.

I rushed to the bed. "Mr. Armstrong," I whispered, as if speaking too loud would wake him. The blood pooled beneath him answered my question before I searched for a pulse that wasn't there. After finding no life in him, I dug my cell phone from my pocket and dialed 911. My fingers shook so badly I had to dial three times before an operator answered. I lowered herself to the edge of the bedside chair.

"911. What is your emergency?"

"Mr. Armstrong is dead?"

"Excuse me? Could you speak louder please?"

"Mr. Armstrong is dead!" Tears burned the back of my throat. No more morning coffee. No more chats about life. What would I do without the father figure I had come to depend on?

"Give me your address, please, and stay on the line."

I nodded, then realizing the operator couldn't see me, mumbled an okay and gave the address. Moses was pacing the gray tile of the bathroom floor. Who would care for the funny animal now?

Approaching footsteps announced I was no longer alone. "Someone's here. I gotta go." I hung up and raced to the closet, pulling the door closed, leaving just enough room to peer out, as a tall man in a business suit entered the room.

Brad Armstrong stopped beside the bed and stared for several seconds before glancing at the closet. Could he hear my breathing? My heart beating?

He placed his fingers on his father's carotid, then caressed the older man's face. With a choking sob, he shook his head, then knelt, leaning his forehead against the mattress before reaching for the bedside phone.

What sort of killer prayed next to his victim?

Moses stopped pacing, sniffed the air, and shot past the stranger into the hall. I slammed the closet open and raced after the orange tabby.

"Wait!" Footsteps pounded behind me.

I scooped up the cat and made a run for the front door.

Brad grabbed my arm, spinning me around to face him. "Did you kill my father?"

"No … I wouldn't. You have a reason to want him dead, not me."

"Of all the silly—"

Sirens wailed in the distance. The cavalry was coming. All I needed to do was stay alive long enough for them to arrest the man in front of me.

"Come inside." He dragged me after him.

It was all I could do to hold onto the hissing, squirming cat and keep up with the man's furious pace. I made a futile kick at his legs, which he easily dodged. "Let go of me."

"Not until I receive some answers." He shoved me toward the sofa. "Now, talk."

The brightest hazel eyes I'd ever seen glared down at her, despite the flicker of sorrow in them. A muscle ticked in his jaw. Quite a handsome killer, this man.

"I'm not talking to anyone except the police." I lifted my chin and tried to look unafraid while keeping a death grip on one very unhappy feline.

He crossed his arms. "Fine by me. They should be here any second. Is that my father's cat?"

"This cat belongs to Mr. Armstrong, yes."

"You may keep it. The cat seems to like you and can't stand me. Never could."

"It's your cologne. Were you here earlier? The place reeks of it." I narrowed my eyes. "Why is that? Do you hate cats? Were you cruel to him?"

"Of course not." He turned at the pounding on the door and hurried to let the authorities in. "My father's body is in the bedroom."

Two police officers and two paramedics rushed past them. Another officer, an Officer McIlroy, stood guard at the door. "Please sit down." He motioned to the alleged son. "Name?"

"Brad Armstrong. The victim is my father."

"Did you find the body? The 911 call came from a woman."

"That would be me, Trinity Ashford. Mr. Armstrong met me for coffee every morning and dropped off his cat. I own Tail-Waggin' Love Pet Day Care. When he didn't show up this morning, I got worried." The tears I'd held in escaped, running down my cheeks and dripping onto Moses's fur. "The door was open. I came in and … found him."

Spotting a pet carrier in the corner behind an easy chair, I stood and placed Moses inside the carrier. My arms were already sporting several scratches, and I couldn't take any more of the cat's hissing at Brad before I lost what little of my mind or skin remained.

Brad glanced at me, his brow furrowed. "I was supposed to meet my father here this morning to discuss some changes to the company. The front door was open, and this woman was hiding in the closet."

"Because you might be the killer!" I plopped on the sofa as far from him as I could get.

"Don't be ridiculous. Why would I kill him?" Tears shimmered in his amazing eyes.

I almost lost myself in them. Almost. "I don't know, but I plan to find out." I wiped my face on the sleeve of my tee shirt.

"Are either of you planning on leaving town

anytime soon?" The officer asked.

I shook my head. "I have a business to run. It doesn't allow for much free time."

Brad sighed. "No. I'm here for quite a while now. My father and I were going to be working together."

"Strange that I've never heard of you." I glanced toward the bedroom. The kind Mr. Armstrong had not once mentioned a son during our time together. I caught the flash of a camera and shuddered.

"It doesn't mean I don't exist."

The officer glanced from one to the other and shook his head. "We'll be taking both of you to the station for questioning."

"I'm a suspect?" A sob erupted.

"You're both persons of interest." Clearly the officer didn't know how to handle a distraught woman. He paled and took a step back.

"My father has just been murdered, and you're treating me like a criminal?" Brad cleared his throat and turned his head, his voice lowering. "There is so much planning to do."

"You have time. The body won't be released for a few days." Officer McIlroy moved to the front door. His dark-eyed gaze stayed locked on the two of us on the sofa.

It was all a nightmare. First, I'd lost the best friend I had in the world other than Heather, and now I was a suspect in his death. I reached for a tissue in a nearby box and blew my nose. "There is a witness to the murder."

"What?" Both men spoke at once.

"Moses, the cat." I squared my shoulders and leaned closer to get a good whiff of Brad. "The cat only hisses when it smells a certain brand of cologne. The same cologne Brad Armstrong wears." I lifted my chin and offered a triumphant grin.

"That's ridiculous." Brad's eyes widened. "This is a very popular scent."

I shrugged. "Nevertheless, cats don't lie."

"Miss Ashford." Officer McIlroy slid the notebook into his breast pocket. "A cat is not a substantial witness."

"He's more reliable than most people." How could they not understand? Moses was a very personable cat. If he disliked a certain type of person, he'd make the perfect witness. "I smelled the cologne myself when I entered this apartment, and I smelled it again when Brad came in. The killer wears this particular cologne. I'd swear on it."

"For crying out loud." Brad slumped on the sofa. "You're making a mockery of my father's murder."

"I wouldn't dare. I loved him too much." The waterworks started again, and I reached for another tissue. "You killed your father, and I intend to prove it."

Chapter 4

After a grueling day at the police station, I arrived home and released Moses from his carrier. He shot under my bed, ignoring Trashcan and Sharkbait, who were happy to see their friend, at least I thought they were happy to see him.

Several notes from unhappy customers had been left under the door. Suspecting there would be many more in emails, I booted up my computer and sent out a mass email stating I'd had a family emergency and was sorry for the inconvenience. Hopefully, the unhappy people would be back. If I ever wanted to accumulate the funds to attend veterinary school, I needed every dollar.

Plus, the police still refused to consider poor Moses a witness. I turned off the computer and headed for my small apartment kitchen, tamping my sorrow down. The muted barking of dogs drifted upstairs, reminding me I needed to tend to the poor puppies boarded with me. After feeding the three cats, I moved downstairs and flicked on the light.

"Playtime." I strolled down the aisle of cages, opening doors so the animals could run around the fenced yard. While they romped, I filled food and water dishes, doing my best to shove the horror of the day to the back of my mind.

How could the police actually think me a suspect? Ridiculous. If anyone was a suspect it was Brad Armstrong. He wore the cologne the apartment reeked of. Of course, I thought he smelled delicious, but Moses didn't.

I shook thoughts about handsome Brad from my mind. He was here to ruin my life. Thinking about him in any capacity other than trouble would not work in my favor. Besides, I had my life planned out...work and someday, school. Even more pressing issues were clearing my name and helping put Mr. Armstrong's killer behind bars.

"Sorry I'm late. My child decided not to cooperate this morning." Heather rushed into the kennel area.

"No worries. I was late, too."

My friend's eyes widened. "You're never late."

"Oh, Heather, I've had a horrible morning." Tears streamed down my face. "Mr. Armstrong is dead."

Heather didn't hesitate to lead me to the front of the store and help me into a chair before sitting across from me. "I'm so sorry to hear that. How did he die?"

"He was murdered, and the police think I did it."

"What?" She covered her mouth with her hand.

"Well, me or his son, Brad."

23

"Tell me what happened."

I explained every minute of what had transpired in Mr. Armstrong's penthouse. "Moses hates that cologne. I'm sure he saw the killing happen and can identify the killer."

"If only he could talk."

"We'll watch the cat real close. If he acts funny around someone, we'll have our suspect."

"What do you mean *we*?" Heather shook her head. "Leave this to the police. I can't go hunting a murderer. I have a child, and Bobby would kill me himself."

"I'm just saying we keep our eyes and ears open, paying special attention to Moses."

"Where is the cat?"

"Upstairs. I only have three months to prove Brad killed his father or my rent goes up. You know I can't afford that."

"I did not kill my father."

We both gasped to see Brad standing in the doorway. I'd been so engrossed in my conversation with my friend I hadn't heard the bell over the door jingle.

"But I am glad to hear you're going to snoop around." He pulled up a chair and straddled it. He wasn't wearing any cologne this time. "If we work together, we'll find out what really happened and can turn the information over to the police."

I stared at him as if he were a three-eyed coon. "What makes you think I want to work with you? You're here to ruin my life."

"Can we set that aside for now, please?" Pain etched his face. "Someone killed my father. It wasn't me, and I don't believe it was you."

That was something at least. "You're right. I'm sorry. Do you have a plan?"

"I'll work the store and you two head back to your office," Heather said. "This isn't something that needs to be discussed in the open. I've got some time before I have to pick up Robbie."

"Good idea." I stood and motioned for Brad to follow me to my modest office containing a battered wooden desk, an office chair, a straight-backed chair, and a filing cabinet. The walls were covered with photos of cats and dogs.

Brad took a quick glance around, then sat in the straight-backed chair. At least he didn't comment on my office, which was more than likely substandard to his.

Sitting in the office chair, I folded my hands on the desktop. "Let me ask again. Do you have a plan?"

"No." He crossed his arms. "This is your town. Where does someone go to find information?"

"Information or gossip? Because if it's gossip you want, Style Yourself is the town grapevine."

"I'm thinking you need a haircut." He grinned.

"Maybe." I fought not to smile back and lost. "Even a nugget of truth might give us a lead. Also, someone in his apartment complex had to see a stranger enter the building. That's also something we could check into. Are you staying there?"

He shook his head, his smile fading. "It's a crime scene. I'm at the motel."

"That's probably not up to your standards."

"I'm not a snob, Trinity. Why do you dislike me

so much? We only met yesterday."

"I've already told you why."

"I could just as easily say you were manipulating my father's kindness." His look hardened. "But, I'd rather work with you than against you. People around here will talk to you better than they will me. I'm a stranger."

"Okay." They would revisit the subject of rising rent in three months. I reached for the phone on my desk and made a hair appointment. When I'd finished, I turned my attention back to Brad. "Why would someone want your father dead?"

"If everyone else in this strip mall feels the same as you about change, my guess is one of them. How would they know Dad wasn't on the same page as I was?"

"Let's make a list." I pulled a pad of paper from a desk drawer. "There's Mrs. Hedford of the salon, but I can't picture her as a killer. Mr. Mills with the hardware store, Mrs. Murdock runs the thrift shop, Mr. and Mrs. Parker own the drugstore, and Mrs. Ansley the bookstore...I can't see any of them doing this."

"Someone did. What about the apartment complex?"

"I don't know those people as well. That building sticks out like a rich thumb in this town, all glass and concrete rather than brick and wood siding. Besides Mr. Appleton, who lets me in, I don't know anyone there."

"Imagine the rest of Waterfall as new and modern as that building."

I shuddered. "God forbid we lose the small-town feel." Which had started with the construction of Waterfall Apartments.

"We've got a plan of sorts. You get a haircut, we question the other shop owners, the concierge, and anyone else at the apartments we can convince to speak with us. Someone knows something. It's up to us to find out what."

"So, we're going with the motive of forced change for the murder?" I frowned. "Sounds too simple."

"For now. Once I can enter my father's place, I'll dig around in his records. See if he had a secret."

"Why were the two of you estranged?" I cocked her head.

"It's personal."

"Your father said it happened when your mother died."

"I said it's personal." He stood. "Let me know what you find out at the salon." He marched from my office.

I returned to the kennels to usher the dogs back into their cages. My hair appointment was for right after work. Not that I really needed one, but a trim wouldn't hurt. Especially if I gathered some information.

Once the store closed, I told Heather goodnight, grabbed my purse, and headed to Style Yourself.

"Hello, Mrs. Hedford."

"How many times have I asked you to call me Millie?" The early-forties woman smiled. "Sit. I'm ready for you."

I sat, placing my purse on the counter. All four

chairs in the salon were full. Hopefully, that would get a good conversation going.

"Did you hear about poor Mr. Armstrong?" Millie clasped the apron around my neck. "Tragic. Simply tragic."

"I found his body." I choked on the words.

"You poor dear." Millie clicked her tongue. "I know the two of you were close."

"We were." My eyes stung. I wasn't having to act.

"Word on the street is his son did the deed." Millie picked up a pair of scissors. "What are we doing today?"

"How about some layers?" I could do with a new look, and a new cut might help ease the pain in my chest. "I thought at first the son might have, too, but he doesn't have a motive."

A woman in another chair swiveled. "Of course, he does. He wants to change the town and not for the better. Mr. Armstrong was completely against it."

"Not completely," another hairdresser said. "He did okay with that monstrosity of an apartment building. I heard Mr. Armstrong was in complete support of the whole thing. He lived in the penthouse after all. Not such a hardship, and he definitely didn't show remorse for tearing down the building. That thing towers over everything. I can't see the mountain from my kitchen window anymore."

I stared at the woman through the mirror. Perhaps Mr. Armstrong wasn't as loved by the townspeople as I'd thought.

"Let's not speak ill of the dead," Millie said, spritzing my head with water. "We've more important things to worry about, like the changing of Waterfall Mall. That young Armstrong might be easy on the eyes, but he's hard on the pocketbook. I'm sorry for his loss, but I can't afford a raise in rent."

The others echoed Millie's statement.

"I heard Mr. Mills say he'd run the man out of town before he'd let him raise his rent," one customer said. "Said if he continued with the changes, something bad would happen."

That was interesting. I would have to make Mr. Mills the next person I questioned. Could Brad's life be in danger?

My mind whirled with questions. Mr. Armstrong said he wouldn't raise rents, Brad said they'd be raised, Mr. Armstrong was murdered, and Brad threatened him in a roundabout way. What was really going on?

"There." Millie handed me a mirror so I could see the back of my head.

"I love it." The layers framed my face, tumbling past my shoulders and showcasing my light brown eyes. "You're a magician."

"Your hair is so lovely it's easy to work with."

I couldn't get my mind off the possible danger to Brad. As I headed to my apartment, I glanced at the hardware store. Portly Mr. Mills didn't seem dangerous, although he wasn't one of the friendliest people I'd ever met. Switching directions, I entered the hardware store. A few men browsed the shelves.

Mr. Mills glanced up from his place behind the

register. "What can I help you with, Trinity?"

"Oh, uh…" I should have thought of a reason for being here. "Nails. Yeah. I need the small ones like you hang pictures with."

He glowered and plucked a box off the shelf behind him. "New hairdo?"

"Yep. Just now." I patted my head. "Did you hear about Mr. Armstrong?"

"Who hasn't? You know how word spreads in this town. Not a great loss for anyone but you and that meddling son of his, if you ask me." He rang up the nails and held out his hand for the money. "I saw him at your store earlier. Mark my words, girlie. If that man gets his way, you'll be out of a place to live and a job."

"There are other storefronts with apartments over them." I dropped a five-dollar bill in his hand and waited for my change. "Maybe not as reasonably priced, but I'll make do. A lot can happen in three months."

"You should use your womanly wiles to convince that man not to do this thing he's come to do."

"Mr. Mills!" My mouth dropped open. Anyone who knew me knew I wasn't the type to use my feminine anything to get what I wanted.

"Suit yourself. Trouble is a' coming."

Chapter 5

"You might be in trouble," I said to Brad the moment he entered the store the next morning, carrying a cardboard container holding three coffees. Seeing how he kept up the tradition his father had sent a pang through my heart.

"Nice hair. How so?" Brad handed me a coffee and set one on the counter for the once-again late Heather.

"How did you know about the coffee?"

"I saw the cups when I was here yesterday morning." He shrugged. "Figured my father had something to do with keeping you supplied. Now, what makes you think I'm in trouble?"

I passed on what I'd heard at the salon and from speaking with Mr. Mills. "That sounds like a threat to me."

"It's no surprise I'm not well-liked. Doesn't mean someone wants to hurt me." He leaned against the counter.

"They felt strongly enough about something to kill your father."

He paled. "Point taken. I'll be careful. What time do you want to make the rounds today and ask some questions." He idly petted Sharkbait who purred and rubbed against him. "This is a big tabby."

"He's mine." My chest swelled with pride. "Sharkbait is a big baby."

Brad laughed. "Strange name."

"My other cat is Trashcan. He used to like sleeping in the trash can I tossed my lint and dryer sheets in. They don't come to their name anyway. Might as well call them something clever." I glanced up as Mrs. Nelson brought in Greta. "Good morning."

"Nothing good about it so far." She stared at Brad. "Had a flat tire this morning. Are you the one causing all the ruckus around here?"

"Guilty." His lips twitched.

"Well, cut it out." She set Greta's carrier on the floor. "She can go out to play today but only for a little while. If she gets dirty, I expect you to return her to me clean."

"Of course." I kept a smile on my face, despite the ruckus the dog caused when Moses tried swatting at her through the carrier door.

"That animal is a nuisance." Mrs. Nelson glared at the cat. "I do hope my baby doesn't get scratched."

"Moses is declawed, ma'am." I scooped up the cat and set him on the counter. "He only wants to play."

"Hmmph." She turned her glare to Brad, turned up her nose, and sailed from the shop.

"Friendly woman." He took a sip of his coffee. "When's a good time for you to leave?"

"Once Heather arrives. There aren't a lot of jobs today, but I do need to spend time finding a way to make more income from this place."

"I'm in advertising. I could help you."

"You'd do that for me?" I widened my eyes. "I can't pay you."

He sighed. "I'm not asking for payment. What services do you offer?"

"Boarding, day care, pet supply sales, and I'd like to hire a groomer."

"I'd hire the groomer first thing if you have what you need to offer that service. You'd make back the person's salary in no time. They could start out part-time. You'd offer introductory prices at first—give an incentive for the owners to use you." He straddled a chair.

"Good idea. What else?"

"Have a two-for-one sale on whatever product sells the most poorly. That way, you can replace it with something more popular." He folded his arms on the chair's back. "People around here love their pets. Hand out a treat when the pets leave." He held up a hand as I opened my mouth to protest. "I know it all costs money, but you have to spend money to make money."

"You're right. Heather's said the same thing. I'll put an ad in the help-wanted section of the paper today, and we do have the equipment. I've considered this before but never got around to hiring anyone." Interviews would take up a lot of my time. "I could use some of the funds I've been saving for veterinary school to pay for these things until the money starts rolling in." Please, God, let the money roll in.

"You want to be a vet?" Brad arched a brow.

"Ever since I was a child." My dream kept getting pushed further and further away. Maybe I should focus my efforts on the shop and forget my future.

"Sorry I'm late." Heather fought with the door and a stroller. "Babysitter called in sick." Robbie kicked and screamed. "Shh, you can play with the puppies."

"Let me." Brad unbuckled the two-year-old and plopped him on the counter. "What's all the fuss? What little boy wouldn't want to play with puppies?" He tapped his forefinger on the boy's nose, who grinned and stopped making a fuss. "You be good and let your momma work."

I exchanged a shocked look with Heather, then turned back to Brad. "You're good with him."

"Why so surprised? I like kids." He set Robbie on the floor. "Mind if I steal Trinity for a while, Heather? We'd like to ask some questions of the other tenants."

"Sure. I'll call if I get in a bind." She didn't look pleased, but corralling a toddler and animals wouldn't be an easy task. I filled her in on plans for the shop. "Great. I'll work on fliers if I have time. If you haven't contacted the paper yet, I'll do that."

"Thank you. You're a lifesaver." I flashed a

smile and followed Brad out the door as Heather grabbed her coffee.

As we passed the empty store next to mine, I said, "Instead of raising rent, why don't you try filling the two empty stores in this mall? Both are big enough for either a grocery or department store."

He chuckled. "Looks like I'm not the only one with ideas."

I shrugged. It made sense to me. "Plus, the mall could use a facelift. New paint and such. No need to run us all off, and that's what will happen if you raise the rent. Then, you'll have an empty mall." I chewed my pinkie nail.

He cut me a sideways glance, pulling my hand from my mouth. "I thought we agreed not to talk about this for a while."

"Suit yourself." I stepped aside to let him open the door to Mills' Hardware.

Mr. Mills' look should have frozen us in place. "What do you want?"

Brad strode to the counter, seeming unfazed by the man's rudeness. "I heard you're unhappy with me. Maybe you were unhappy with my father, as well."

"Of course, I am. You're going to mess everything up."

Brad crossed his arms. "Like what?"

"My business. I'm turning a profit, but I won't if overhead goes up."

"How well did you know my father?"

"As well as a tenant knows their landlord. He sure lived high on the hog in that penthouse of his, didn't he? Lording it over us peasants." Mr. Mills glowered.

"Mr. Armstrong wasn't like that at all." I matched his sour expression with one of my own. How dare he criticize that dear man? "He was a kind gentleman who did his best to keep us all happy."

"I don't recall him bringing coffee to me every morning."

"Would that make you happy, Mr. Mills?" Brad raised his brows. "If I brought you coffee each morning?"

"I'd rather not have to look at you."

We were getting nowhere. After a few more seconds of the two men in a stare down, I gripped Brad's sleeve. "We should go."

"You shouldn't consort with the enemy, Missy," Mr. Mills said. "You don't have any enemies in this town, but that might not always be the case."

I whirled. "Are you threatening me?" My blood simmered.

"Only saying what's true. Now, if the two of you are done, I've work to do."

Brad placed his hand on the small of my back, sending tingles through me, and guided me from the store. "Thank you for defending my father."

"I'm fiercely loyal to the people I care about." I cleared my throat. "Next stop, the hair salon. You'll cause quite the stir, being a man and all. They rarely grace the door of the place."

"I'll do my best to contain my excitement." He gave me a dimpled grin.

All conversation ceased when we entered the

shop. Millie rushed toward us, a blush on her round face. "How may I help you two?"

"I'm Brad Armstrong." He held out his hand.

"Everyone here knows exactly who you are." While admiration shone in her eyes, her smile faltered a bit. "I'm surprised to see you with Trinity."

"Why?" His brow furrowed. "We're working together to find out what happened to my father."

"Well, uh, it's because..." She exhaled heavily. "Never mind. Have a seat, although I'm not sure what I can tell you."

"I was told you knew everything that happened in this town." Brad's smile returned. "Surely, you suspect who might have disliked my father enough to kill him."

"Sweetie, your father lost friends the minute he built that apartment complex."

"Why? Who did it directly affect?"

She scrunched up her face. "It increased traffic for one, causing another entrance to the community on the hill. That didn't sit right with folks. Plus, those who live in that highfalutin place tend to shop outside of Waterfall, thinking our shops aren't good enough for them."

So far, there were too many suspects to narrow down. I'd hear the grumblings at the town meetings, but no one seemed angry enough to kill, only annoyed. "Who did Mr. Armstrong purchase the land from?"

"Someone out of state, from what I heard. A lot of outsiders have been buying up the land around here."

"Can you find out who the owner was?" I asked Brad.

"Shouldn't be too hard. Thank you for your time, ma'am."

"You don't seem as awful as people say you are." Millie tilted her head. "Too bad you're in town for all the wrong reasons."

Outside, Brad shook his head. "I'll never be able to shrug off the stigma that I'm here to ruin Waterfall. I'm not. I'd like to improve the living conditions of those who live here."

"What if everyone is happy as things are?" I stared up at him.

"I'm a businessman. It's my job to improve my holdings."

"What are you trying to sell?"

"The apartment complex."

"Why?"

"Dad got us into a bit of…financial trouble. Mismanagement of funds, that kind of thing. I came to straighten everything out."

"Perhaps you should take your own advice, think of my ideas, and spend money to make money." I laughed and continued down the sidewalk.

"Touché, my dear." He left my side and stood in the middle of the parking lot.

I joined him. "What are you doing?"

"Considering your ideas." He studied each storefront, turning in a slow circle.

Joy that he hadn't tossed my suggestions to the wind put a bounce in my step. "What do you see?"

"A mall that could be profitable."

"Without raising rent?"

"Maybe. Paint, new signs, some CCTV cameras."

"We don't have a lot of crime in this town."

His gaze hardened. "We just had a murder. Security cameras might make filling those empty stores easier."

He'd said *we*. Was he planning on staying in town indefinitely?

"I'll head back to Mills and Millie tomorrow and ask what they'd like changed. We can use that as our excuse for visiting the other stores, then ask about my father. His killer is close, breathing down our necks. All we have to do is identify him."

"I'll say it again, we should take Moses with us."

Brad rolled his eyes and turned toward the thrift shop.

Scoff all he wanted, but the cat knew who murdered Mr. Armstrong.

Chapter 6

Murdock's Someone Else's Junk smelled slightly musty. Still, the place felt like home to me as I bought most of my clothes and dishes from there in an attempt to build up my bank account.

"This place could definitely use some sprucing up," Brad whispered.

"Shh. Mrs. Murdock is a widow and does the best she can." I smiled and greeted the elderly lady hanging clothes on wire hangers.

"Good morning, Trinity." Her wrinkled face beamed. "I have some new things in. Just your size, too."

My face heated as Brad glanced my way. "I'll look later. We have some questions for you." Since the woman made the rounds of the town, picking through dumpsters and other people's trash in addition to receiving donations, she knew more about the townspeople than even Millie. "This is Brad Armstrong."

"Oh, everyone knows who he is." Unlike the others, no glint of suspicion flickered in her eyes. "I was sorry to hear about your father. Such a nice man. I'm happy to help in any way I can. How about a casserole?" Her eyes twinkled. "I could drop it off at Trinity's, and the two of you could enjoy a homecooked meal together."

"Thank you." Brad's voice cracked.

The last thing he needed was one of Mrs. Murdock's overcooked casseroles, or I for that matter. "We're wondering if you've heard or seen anything in your trips around town that might help us understand why Mr. Armstrong was murdered."

Mrs. Murdoch pursed her lips. "Could be any number of things, I reckon. The selling of that apartment complex might leave a lot of people without jobs. Then, there's his wanting to change this mall." She shrugged. "Neither one worries me much. I collect a lot of castoffs from those people in that complex. Worse comes to worse, I sell things online and out of my garage." Lowering her voice, she leaned closer. "I've heard Bobby Langley is upset about the possibility of his wife losing her job, even if it's part-time. Money woes."

Why hadn't Heather told me? I could try to tighten my belt and increase her hours. At the very least, I could insist she bring Robbie to work with her more often to save babysitting fees.

I stuck my nose in the air and returned my attention to Mrs. Murdoch. "Thank you for the info. Please let us know if you think of anything else."

"I will, dear. Remember to come back before all the good stuff is gone."

Outside, I hurried to the drugstore tucked away in the corner of the strip mall and shoved the door open. Mr. Parker smiled from where he slid greeting cards into a stand-up rack. "Hello." He didn't spare Brad a glance.

Oops. Not a fan. "Do you have time to answer a few questions?"

"Sure." Now he looked Brad's way before heading toward the back of the store. "What are you looking for?"

"I noticed this is a large space for what few items you carry. Have you considered an old fashioned soda fountain? A bar here with stools, serve sandwiches? If you could draw in the younger crowd, you'd increase your profit."

Mr. Parker and I stared at each other before he answered, "I've considered it but didn't think anyone would be interested."

Brad shrugged. "It's a small town. Don't the teens need a safe place to hang out and bring their dates?"

The drugstore owner's narrowed. "I thought you were here to cause trouble."

"I'm here to increase profit. A little bird told me that improving the businesses already here and finding renters for the vacant storefronts might be a better path to take." He smiled my way.

Okay, I liked him again and forgave him for not being totally upfront. "I'm going to be hiring a dog groomer."

"Why not convert that biggest store to a movie theater? It wouldn't be a very large one, but it would bring in a lot of customers for the rest of us."

Mr. Parker nodded like a bobblehead doll. "Why not form a committee with all of us still here for ideas on improvement? Might convince folks to like you better."

Brad's features hardened. At first, I'd thought maybe public opinion didn't matter much to him. I was wrong. He seemed clearly bothered by the man's comment. "Have you heard anything that might explain someone wanting my father dead?"

"Loss of jobs? Loss of income? Not that I consider those a strong enough motive, but perhaps someone did. Or it could be something else entirely."

I couldn't help but wonder what Mr. Parker might think was a motive for murder but kept my mouth shut. "We'll let you know about the committee."

Back outside, Brad bypassed the bookstore and stood in front of the last storefront that took up half that side of the mall. He glanced up. "If I built a second story, I could have four or five theaters."

"I thought you didn't have any money."

"My father was running out. I have plenty. I came to bail him out and help him move forward." He gave a lopsided grin. "See? I'm a nice guy. I just didn't come across that way at first. Stress makes me...blunt."

That's putting it mildly. "Want to visit the bookstore?"

"Sure. We haven't learned much so far. Then, we can head to the apartments. I feel like we're at an impasse."

"But you're getting to know the tenants. That's

worth something." I still needed to speak with Heather about her husband's alleged money problems.

Mrs. Ansley was too busy to speak with us and had no problem letting us know it. She said she'd be interested in the committee, but as the only bookstore in town, she had inventory to do.

"That's that," I said, strolling at Brad's side back to Tail-Waggin'.

Heather glanced up as we entered. "You have three interviews this afternoon." She glanced at the clock. "The first one in half an hour. All seem highly qualified."

"Good job. May I speak with you in the back?"

"Why so formal?" She frowned.

"Sorry. Just tired." I led her back to the office, knowing we could hear the bell over the door jingle if anyone entered.

"Want me to corral these cats?" Brad called after us. "They're swarming the door."

"Yes, please." I motioned for Heather to have a seat across from me. "We don't have a lot of time, so I'll get right to the point. Are you and Bobby in financial trouble?"

She paled. "He has a gambling problem. I was too embarrassed to tell you. I've been late for work so much because I can't afford to pay the babysitter and had to wait for someone who would watch Robby for free."

"Bring him here with you every day." I held out my hand and gave hers a gentle squeeze. "We'll increase your hours."

"You can't afford that and hire a groomer."

Tears welled in her eyes.

"We'll work it out."

She nodded. "Did you find out any news on Mr. Armstrong?"

I sat back in my chair. "Only that he wasn't as well liked as I thought and that he had plans to sell the apartment complex. Brad has agreed to form a committee of the tenants to come up with ways to improve the property. I'm not sure how that goes with his original plan to make more income other than filling the two vacant stores."

"That would help his books."

"Especially since he plans on turning the one next to the bookstore into a two-story theater. He can charge a ton of rent on that one." I was sick of talking about money. Somehow I had to figure out how to pay a groomer and give Heather more hours. I was on the verge of a crying fest, only to be saved by Brad letting us know the first appointment had arrived early.

Heather left, her seat filled by a girl barely out of high school.

"I'm Amber, and I love animals. I'm solely responsible for washing my mother's Yorkies and feel as if I would be great to work here."

I stifled a sigh. "Any professional experience?"

"Not yet." She grinned.

I thanked her for her time after she told me she'd never worked before and promised to let her know my decision. The next eager interviewee was only slightly better, having worked at a fast-food restaurant, but her heart's desire was to work with animals. Maybe Waterfall didn't have any experienced groomers after all.

"Sorry I'm late." A middle-aged woman plunked a folder on the desk in front of me. "My car, poor thing, has seen better days. Everything you want to know about me is right in front of you." She tapped the folder with a bright red fingernail. "Name is Sharon Lee Carpenter. Friends call me Shar."

A bit overwhelmed by her energy after what was already a long day, I opened the file. She'd actually worked at a grooming place for several years until her husband died and she returned to her hometown.

"You're hired. When can you start? We'll need to set up the back room before officially opening that part of the business." I offered my hand for a shake.

"I can start tomorrow. I'd love to set up that room. That way, it'll be exactly as I like it. Do you want me every day or only a few days a week?"

I widened my eyes. I hadn't thought of part-time, but that would help ease some of the financial burden. "How about a full week to set up the room, then Tuesdays and Thursdays? If we find out business is actually booming, we can increase your days."

"That sounds perfect to me. I do have a flower garden that needs my attention. Wouldn't want to let it lapse." She returned my shake. "I'll be here at eight in the morning. You won't regret this."

Other than feeling tired after only a few minutes with her, I brightened at the thought that this idea might just work. "Let me introduce you to Heather."

Shar followed me to the front of the store.

"This is Heather. She helps with the store and the boarding. This is Brad Armstrong, the landlord."

Her gaze roamed up and down him. "How can such a handsome man have caused such an uproar in town? You need to watch your back, Mr. Armstrong. There are some who think you should meet the same end as your father."

Chapter 7

Brad's usual carved-in-stone expression crumbled. "Why do people think someone wants to kill me next?"

"We'll figure that out when we find your father's killer." How were we going to keep Brad safe until then?

"Let's think about this," Shar said, holding up a finger for each point. "One, folks are scared. Two, well, I don't have a two, but we'll get another reason soon enough. I'll see you tomorrow."

After she breezed out the door, Brad turned to me. "She's so exhausting I need a nap, and you hired her?"

"She was the best qualified." I had no doubt she'd do a good job. "She'll only be working Tuesday and Thursday after the room is set up. Her enthusiasm is refreshing."

"Right." Heather grinned. "Besides, she'll be in the back most of the time." She rubbed her hands together. "I feel good about this."

"What now?" I glanced at Brad. "The store closes in an hour."

"The apartment complex." He glanced at his phone. "The crime scene tape is still up, but I have a key. We'll have to do this quietly."

The bell over the door jingled as Mrs. Nelson entered. My two felines, plus the third stooge, Moses, darted for the open door.

Brad moved like a running back in a football game and headed them off. "Why do you let them run loose? It's only a matter of time before they escape."

"They're indoor cats. They'd freeze the minute their feet hit the sidewalk. Hello, Mrs. Nelson. Greta is ready for you—" I raised an eyebrow at Heather who nodded.

"I'll go get her." My friend disappeared into the back, returning a minute later with the carrier containing a yipping schnauzer. "We'll have an onsite groomer starting next Tuesday and Thursday. I hope you'll consider using us the next time this precious girl needs a cut."

"I certainly will. Much more convenient since she's here all day anyway." A smile actually crossed her face. "Whenever I can save time, it's a wonderful thing. I want to book the first appointment for Tuesday."

After she left the store, I clapped my hands. "Our first grooming customer! Do you have the fliers finished?"

Heather reached under the counter and handed me a stack. "I could only place a small ad in the paper, but it's a start."

"Let's deliver a few to all the stores here, then head to the complex." I smiled at Brad. "Can you lock up, Heather?"

"Yep."

Brad took the fliers and followed me from the shop. "A quick stop and we'll be on our way."

Twenty minutes later, I sat on the buttery leather seats of his Mercedes. I caressed the seat as if touching a baby. What would it be like to afford such luxury? "Your car is gorgeous."

"Do you have a boyfriend?""

I frowned. "No, why? I'm far too busy."

"Because you're stroking that leather seat as a woman might caress the face of her lover." He winked and turned the key in the ignition.

My face heated. The way his eyes had darkened almost made me think he was jealous of the seat, but that was ridiculous. We'd just met and not under the best circumstances.

In front of the complex, a valet took the car once we'd stepped out. Brad placed his hand on the small of my back and guided me into the building.

"Hello, Mr. Appleton." I greeted the doorman. "You've met Mr. Armstrong, I presume."

His eyes narrowed "We've met briefly. Have the authorities released the penthouse?"

Without answering, Brad continued to the elevator. I supposed no answer was slightly better than an outright lie. He pressed the number for the penthouse. Yellow crime scene tape waved as we stepped off the elevator. Careful not to pull it down, Brad held it up so I could duck under, then followed me. "I want to search the place really well now that we're here without authorities breathing down our necks."

True. I still hadn't gotten over the suspicion in Officer McIlroy's eyes.

Brad stopped inside so abruptly my nose pressed against his back.

"Sorry," I mumbled, rubbing my nose. "What's wrong?"

"I can't believe he's gone." His voice cracked.

"Me either." I slipped my hand in his. "We can wait to do this another time."

"No. I need to know what happened here." He gave my hand a squeeze and pulled free, marching toward the bedroom, his back straight.

We stopped in the doorway. My gaze locked on the stained mattress. The sheets and blankets had been removed, but blood had seeped through them.

Brad whirled and strode to the kitchen. "The killer used one of Dad's own knives. I gave the set to him for Christmas. One of the best." He turned to me, his eyes red. "Tell me about the man my father had become."

"How long has it been since you've seen him?"

"Over five years. We had the occasional phone call but stuck to business. I sent him gifts for Christmas and his birthday. That's it." He lowered to a stool at the kitchen island.

I sat on the one next to him. "He was kind, at least to me. Said I was the daughter he'd always wanted. I had no idea there were people who didn't care for him. He loved animals and donated regularly to the animal shelter and other local charities. Maybe that's where his money went?"

"No, charitable donations were in the budget. He lost his money to poor business decisions, like not keeping the strip mall full of tenants." Brad folded his hands in his lap. "You were right about work needing to be done. I had no idea how much, though."

"We'll work with the tenants to get it done."

He exhaled heavily and stood. "We aren't accomplishing anything by sitting here. Which room do you want to search?"

"For?"

"Clues. Anything that might help us find his killer."

"I'll take the bedroom." I didn't really want to, but the look of relief on his face spurred me on. Leaving him in the kitchen, I returned to the bedroom, averting my gaze from the spot on the mattress.

Instead, I dropped to my knees and glanced under the bed. Something had once been placed there and removed considering the fine film of dust had been disturbed. Hadn't Mr. Armstrong hired a maid? I thought the complex provided one for a fee. I pushed to my feet and entered the office.

Bookshelves filled the walls. It didn't look as if a book was missing, but how would I know? No laptop or desktop computer sat on the polished cherrywood desk. Most likely, the police had confiscated it as potential evidence.

"Find anything?" Brad spoke behind me.

"Something used to be under the bed, but it isn't there now. Didn't your father have a maid? There's dust under there." I turned to face him. "I can't tell if anything other than his computer is missing from here. I really didn't visit him much. He brought me coffee each morning. That's when we visited."

His brow furrowed. "It wasn't like my extremely neat father to have anything under the bed, much less dust. Did you check the closet?"

"Not yet." I brushed past him, savoring a whiff of his cologne. Moses didn't know what he was thinking. The man smelled delicious.

Returning to the bedroom, I entered a closet as big as the bedroom in my tiny apartment. Matching storage boxes lined the shelf above clothes hung in coordinating colors. One rod consisted entirely of suits. Nothing looked out of place. Feeling as if I was violating his privacy, I rifled through the suit pockets and scored on the fourth suit, pulling out a business card for an upscale nightclub from a neighboring town. I had no idea Mr. Armstrong went to such places. I pocketed the card and continued my search with no new leads.

We needed to know what had been stored under the bed but couldn't ask the police if they'd taken it without revealing we'd entered a crime scene without permission.

"Let's talk to the concierge about the lapsing maid service," I said, joining Brad in the living room. "I also found this." I handed him the business card.

"A lot of business transactions take place at this club." He pursed his lips. "Do you have a fancy dress? Cocktail-type? They have a dress code."

I didn't but knew where I could get one. The thrift store always had cocktail dresses, since there wasn't a huge demand for them. So, I nodded.

"Great. We'll go tomorrow night." He pocketed the card. "We're done here, at least for now."

We left the penthouse and approached the concierge's desk, where a tall thin man wearing the name tag of Stevenson met us without smiling. "How may I help you?"

Brad introduced himself. "Did my father use the maid service?"

Stevenson typed on a keyboard. "Yes, until three days ago, then he canceled."

"Did he say why?"

The man shook his head. "He might have mentioned leaving town for a few days, but I heard that from Appleton not from Mr. Armstrong himself."

First I'd heard of it. I glanced to where the doorman watched us, curiosity on his face. I left Brad's side. "Did Mr. Armstrong tell you he planned on leaving town for a few days?"

"Yes. Said he had out-of-town business."

"Did he say where he was going?"

"No, but he did seem...I couldn't tell if it was anxiety or excitement."

Hmmm. He'd seemed normal when I'd seen him and had invited me over. Would he have told me of his plans then, if he'd had the chance?

I thanked Appleton and returned to Brad's side. "Your father seemed rather anxious or excited to the doorman, but he'd appeared normal to me before he died."

Brad took my arm and led me outside. "I don't want to talk too much in front of other people. Let me buy you dinner and we can discuss this further."

I glanced at my jeans and tee-shirt. "Nothing fancy. I know a great burger place."

"Perfect."

Fifteen minutes later, we sat in a red vinyl booth waiting for double bacon cheeseburgers. "Other than the nightclub, I don't know what our next step should be," I said.

"Me either. We'll set up a group meeting for the mall residents for the night after next and visit the club tomorrow evening. We might learn something." He seemed defeated.

"Uh oh. Trouble in a uniform." I motioned my head toward the door of the diner where Officer McIlroy stood, looking around. Spotting us, he strode our way. Even if he'd found out we'd been in the penthouse, he couldn't have known we'd come here, could he?

"Armstrong, Ashford."

"Officer," Brad said. "Can we help you?"

"There's something on your father's computer we'd like to question you about. Can you come to the station after you've finished your meal?"

"What is it?"

"I'd rather not discuss it here." With a definitive nod, he turned and marched from the diner.

"I'm afraid to know what he's found," I said.

"My guess is it has something to do with your low rent."

I stiffened. "Why?"

He shrugged. "I told you that you paid less per square foot than anyone else in the mall. I'd spoken to my father about raising your rent. We argued.

What if he actually did plan to raise it? That moves you up the suspect chain."

"What makes you think it's about rent?"

"A gut feeling. I hope I'm wrong."

Me, too.

Chapter 8

With my heart in my throat, we entered the police station. We waited five minutes before being called into Officer McIlroy's office.

"Sit." He motioned, unsmiling, to two chairs across from him.

I shot Brad a nervous glance and sat, folding my hands to keep from fidgeting. It worked with my hands but not my foot, which bounced like one of those bouncy balls I had as a child.

"What's this about?" Brad leaned forward, his gaze locked on the officer.

Officer McIlroy, wait...no, it's Detective...had I called him Officer before? My face heated as the detective opened a laptop, pressed some keys, and turned the laptop around so we could see the screen.

"This is why the two of you remain my top suspects." He straightened.

"What are we looking at?" It looked like financial records.

Brad sighed and tapped the screen. "Your rent

was going to be raised quite a bit. My father intended to sell the apartment complex to pay off his debts. Whatever money he had left at the time of his death would go to charity." He sat back in his chair. "We both stood to lose a substantial amount of money, if he were alive."

I widened my eyes. "Why would he be preparing for his death all of a sudden?"

"I see you weren't aware your father had pancreatic cancer." Detective McIlroy steepled his fingers. "Or maybe you were and killed him before he could change his will."

"That's ridiculous." Brad's face darkened. "I came here to help him figure out this mess, not take it from him. I had no idea he was ill."

"So you say."

"What do you want from us, Detective?" Brad crossed his arms.

"For you to prove I'm wrong. While you are new in town, Miss Ashford isn't. She's very well-liked in these parts, and I'm getting a lot of pressure from the town's residents. Most of whom think you, sir, are the guilty party."

While it pleased me to know how well-liked I was, I felt bad for Brad. He really was trying to help now that he saw the true state of the tenants and the improvements that were needed in their stores. "We intend to prove our innocence, since it seems you have no other suspects."

The detective narrowed his eyes. "I'd rather you prove your innocence without meddling in my investigation."

"How do you expect us to do that?"

He shrugged. "Show me proof you didn't kill Mr. Armstrong for his money."

"Considering I've hired a groomer and extended the hours of my assistant, it's obvious I am not in financial difficulties." Please don't look at my bank records.

"I have more money than my father, so why would I kill him when we'd just reconciled?"

"Who made the first move?" Detective McIlroy tilted his head.

"I did." Some of Brad's confidence seemed to have dropped.

"Why were you estranged?"

"I withdrew after my mother's murder, and Dad moved on." Brad's tone clearly sounded as if he didn't think this any of the detective's business. "He married again, but it only lasted a year. I was angry that he could love again so soon. I was a kid, just graduated high school, went to college and rarely returned home. Then, Dad moved here, and I experienced all that anger again until I realized time was passing, and I'd been a fool."

My heart ached for Brad, and I slipped my hand in his. "A lot of kids would have acted the same way." I hadn't known Mr. Armstrong had been married twice. Seemed I didn't know much about my friend at all.

"Touching story, Mr. Armstrong." McIlroy folded his hands on his desk. "Don't leave town."

"I'll be here for a while. I'm renovating the Waterfall Mall. When will the penthouse be released?"

"The tape will be removed today. Your plans?"

"I'll clean it out and sell or rent the penthouse."

"Not selling the complex?"

"I haven't thought that far ahead. I'd rather keep my father's assets if I can." Brad stood, pulling me to my feet. "We'll keep searching for that proof you seek." Without a farewell, we marched outside. "I don't understand how he can think one of us killed my father."

"Because he doesn't have a clue who did, and he's grasping at anything." It became more imperative we find out something pertaining to the murder before one of us was arrested for lack of anyone else in custody. "What if I smuggle Moses into the country club tomorrow night? Maybe he'll smell that cologne he hates."

"And get us kicked out?" Brad arched a brow. "Cats are not reliable witnesses, Trinity."

"Moses is." I refrained from stomping my foot. "If we find out who wears the cologne—other than you—and knows your father and has something to lose, we find his killer."

"You're like a bulldog gnawing on a bone." His smile took some of the sting out of his words. "A very cute bulldog."

I laughed. "Thanks for a very busy day, but I need to go home." I'd be busy helping Shar in the morning and finding a dress for the evening.

~

I was nowhere near ready for the energetic Shar first thing in the morning. The woman oozed way too much excitement. I stared at her over the rim of my coffee cup, willing myself to wake up before the doors opened at nine to the public. I wouldn't be able to handle them and my new groomer unless fully alert.

Shar stood, hands on her hips. and stared at the room. "A stainless-steel sink, a drain in the floor in one corner for bathing large dogs, a stainless steel table for grooming...I'm going to need shampoo and such."

"We carry all you need in the front of the store. Take what you need. Just write them down so we can remove the items from inventory."

She marched to a wall spigot with a water hose. "Move back unless you want to get wet. I'm going to spray this whole place down, then disinfect."

"Everything is where you want it?" I thought she might want to move things around.

"I'll know more whether it works when I start working on actual dogs." She turned the hose on full blast, sending me scurrying from the room.

A yowling sent me back to rescue a now drenched Moses, who had taken cover under the table.

"Sorry. I didn't see him until it was too late." Shar grinned and continued spraying everything in sight.

"You poor thing." I grabbed a towel from the supply cabinet and rubbed Moses dry. "I sure wish you could talk, buddy. Brad and I could really use your help." Somehow, I'd find a way to get Moses around people and watch his reaction. The problem was, I didn't have any idea how. It wasn't like I could parade him around on a leash where a lot of men hung out.

"Good morning." Heather fought with the door,

trying to push her stroller in. "I got it," she said, as I made a move to help her. "I'm used to needing three arms."

"Good morning." I set Moses on the counter, turning from Heather to Brad, who entered with four coffees. Bless his heart for continuing his father's morning ritual.

"I can't stay." He handed me a cup, a crooked smile gracing his face. "The tape is off the penthouse. There's a lot to do in order to have the place ready for its next tenant."

"Why don't you stay there?" I took an appreciative sniff of the mocha-flavored coffee.

He shrugged. "Maybe I'll change my mind, but living where my father was murdered…"

Yeah, that might be difficult. "It's paid for and has to be better than the motel." Yes, I'd live there, despite the circumstances, to save a buck. But then, I wasn't wealthy.

"There is a guest room. We'll see." He handed Heather her coffee and sailed out the door with his. Guess the fourth was for Shar.

"I don't know how we ever thought him a bad guy," my friend said. "He remembered our new employee."

"He is a sweetheart. I'm heading to the thrift store for a cocktail dress. I won't be gone long."

"Oh?" She tilted her head. "A hot date?"

"No." My face heated. "We're going to the country club to ask questions. I have to dress the part."

"So you say." She ducked when I threw a dog chew toy at her.

I left the store with her laughter ringing behind me. Say what she would, tonight was not a date. I didn't date. I was too busy working. And too exhausted at the end of the day.

Mrs. Murdoch popped up from behind the counter when I entered. "You're early."

"I need a cocktail dress and shoes."

"Oh, goody. You're venturing out. I have just the thing." She led me to a rack in the back of the store and pulled a ruffled pink dress from a hanger. "This is your size."

"It's hideous." I shuddered. "Don't you have something simple…and black?"

She sighed and replaced the dress. "Must you be boring, dear?" She pulled a stylish black sheath dress from the hanger. "I suppose you could make this look good."

The dress was elegant in its simplicity, and I fell in love with the soft sheen of the fabric. "Shoes?"

"Over here."

I found a pair of kitten heels with a peep toe in my size, then headed for the jewelry counter. A pearl necklace called my name until I saw the price tag.

"Close your mouth before something flies in. I'll let you borrow it. There's matching earrings."

I shook my head. "How about I pay you ten dollars a week?" I'd have it paid off in five weeks and not feel the pinch so much. No way was I letting this go. "I've never owned anything so beautiful. Is it real?"

"I wouldn't sell a donated necklace for that much if it weren't. It's still a fraction of what it would cost new. I'm glad it's going to you. Installment is fine. Now, go try everything on." She handed me the jewelry from the locked case and gave me a gentle shove toward the dressing rooms.

A few minutes later, I stared at the stranger in the mirror. I'd never felt so pretty. The dress skimmed my hips as if made for me. The pumps were as cute as a dog's nose, and the jewelry lent an air of sophistication I never thought I'd feel. Nope, I wouldn't feel out of place at the country club at all.

Mrs. Murdoch ooh'ed and ah'ed when she saw me. "Oh, that man's eyes are going to bug out of his head." She fanned her face. "You look like a movie star. How are you going to wear your hair—up, right?"

I laughed. "Yes." A simple French twist would do.

After changing back into my usual attire of jeans and a tee shirt, I paid and waited while Mrs. Murdoch slid a plastic bag over the dress. "There you go. Have fun. I still think you would have looked lovely in the pink."

"No, thanks. Maybe on Halloween." I left the store with a bounce in my step and hurried to show Heather what I'd purchased.

"I wish I could have a night out." She frowned and leaned against the counter. "A toddler and no money means rented movies and microwave popcorn."

"If I wasn't helping Brad find out who killed his father, I wouldn't be going out either." I hurried upstairs to hang the dress in my closet, then returned to check on Shar.

The grooming room sparkled. She'd even peeled the paper off the window that separated the front of the store from the grooming station. Since we weren't using it, I saw no reason to let our customers know it existed. Now, the room would lure clients in droves, I hoped.

"The place looks great." I smiled.

"Yes, it does." Shar stood by my side. "It didn't take me a week after all. See you Tuesday." And just like that, she left me with my mouth hanging open.

Chapter 9

"Wow." Brad's eyes widened when he arrived to pick me up. "I'll have the prettiest woman in the country as my escort tonight."

My face flushed. While I knew I'd never looked so good, it warmed my heart to hear him say the words. Brad looked good enough to eat in his dark suit and tie. He crooked his arm. I slid mine in his and let him lead me to his waiting Mercedes.

Half an hour later, he pulled up to the Silver Brook Country Club in the neighboring large city. A valet opened the door for me, then caught the keys Brad tossed to him. With his hand on the small of my back, sending tingles up my spine from his warm touch, Brad guided me into the brightly lit clubhouse and straight to the bar and restaurant where a hostess seated us in a cozy nook.

"We'll have to mingle in order to find out anything," Brad said, "but I thought you might want to eat first."

"Thank you." My stomach rumbled in response.

I hadn't known for sure whether we'd have dinner but figured there would be appetizers, so I hadn't eaten since lunch. I ordered a salmon salad and glanced at the other diners. "So, where will mingling take place?"

"The bar and outside area." Brad handed the waitress his menu after ordering a steak and baked potato. "This is the place to be if you have money lining your pockets. A lot of business happens at this club. If my father was wheeling and dealing, we'll find out."

My main objective was to find someone wearing the same expensive scent Brad wore. Other than that, I didn't have a clue what to ask anyone and would follow Brad's lead. "Did you get a lot done at the penthouse?"

"Yeah. I moved in. You're right. Why spend money when there's a perfectly fine guestroom to stay in? I'll decide what to do with the place when we find my father's killer."

My heart hiccupped at the thought of him leaving. I'd gotten used to seeing him every day and hated the thought of another Armstrong man erased from my life.

We made idle chit-chat until our food arrived. I placed my linen napkin in my lap and picked up my fork, staring at the salad on my plate. An inexplicable sadness replaced my hunger. Strange how I didn't want someone I'd just met to leave.

I glanced up as a familiar guy strode through the dining room and out to the patio. What was Bobby doing here? He was the last person I thought we'd see here.

"Strange when the man is broke," Brad said, his gaze following Bobby. "Maybe he's making a deal with someone. A job?"

"Maybe, but Heather hasn't mentioned him switching jobs." Bobby didn't possess a lot of skills that I knew of, other than mechanics. I ate, my attention on my best friend's husband as he approached an older man. Seconds later, the two appeared to be arguing.

"Who is that?"

"Richard Roberts. He owns a lot of second-hand car lots. I've heard tell he's a bit unscrupulous, but that could be just rumors." Still, I'd learned that rumors always held a seed of truth to them. Did Heather know where her husband was tonight?

When we finished eating, Brad held out his hand to help me from the booth. We strolled onto the patio and met Bobby's startled gaze.

"Hey, Trinity." He paled. "Fancy seeing you."

"I'm just as surprised to see you." I smiled, then glanced at the man next to him and held out my hand. "Trinity Ashford. I own Tail-Waggin' in Waterfall."

Roberts raised my hand to his lips instead of shaking it and left me feeling as if I needed a shower from the lecherous glint in his eyes. "My pleasure."

I slipped my hand free. "May we speak with you, Bobby?"

He swallowed hard and nodded, following Brad and me to a section of the patio with fewer people. "I do some work for Roberts."

"That answers one question," I said. "I heard

you're having some money issues. Gambling? And that you've been bad-mouthing the late Mr. Armstrong."

"Who hasn't? You would have had to close shop. Heather and I are already on the verge of losing our house. If she doesn't work, we're destitute. That's why I've taken on extra work from Roberts."

"Doing what?"

"Fixing engines on used cars. What else?" He crossed his arms and backed up. "What business is all this of yours?"

"She's helping me find out what happened to my father." A tic showed in Brad's jaw. "We're questioning everyone who had a beef with my father."

"Then you've scored big time. A lot of people were upset with him for one reason or another."

"Mr. Roberts?" I raised my brows.

He lowered his voice. "Yes, but I don't know why."

I narrowed my eyes and pulled him behind a large potted plant. "You're lying."

"Good grief, woman, give me a break. You may be my wife's boss, but you aren't mine." He yanked his arm free. "Mind your own business before you get in trouble. You don't know the type of people you're dealing with."

"That needs an explanation." Brad's hard tone interrupted us.

Bobby took a deep breath and exhaled slowly. "Take my word for it. There are things going on here you don't want to be involved in." He skittered away, almost running across the golf course.

I turned and stared into Roberts' cold gaze. My heart skipped a beat. If looks could kill, I'd be six feet under. "What now?" I whispered to Brad.

"We mingle." He crooked his arm.

I hooked mine with his and pasted a polite smile on my face as we strolled past Roberts. The only reason I could come up with for his hateful glare was that he'd overheard our conversation with Bobby and had something to do with what we were warned to stay out of. "You need a used car."

"Really? I thought you liked the Mercedes." Brad grinned.

"I love it. You can always resell the used one or just go browsing. Roberts warrants a closer look. Know anyone who can dig into his background?"

"Not really. I'm just a businessman, remember? Not law enforcement."

Too bad. I supposed I could pretend to be in search of a car. Mine had seen better days, but since I rarely went anywhere, it served my needs.

"Mr. Armstrong." A silver-haired man stepped into our path. "My condolences on your loss."

"Thank you. I'm sorry, but I don't know who you are."

The man seemed surprised. "Really? Your father and I have been in negotiations over the apartment complex for months. I'm Harold Jenkins. Construction."

"I wasn't aware negotiations were in progress." Brad squared his shoulders. "It'll take me some time to dig through his reports. Do you have a card?"

Jenkins pulled a business card from an inside pocket of his jacket and dropped it into Brad's open hand. "I understand. Give me a call when you've got the time."

"I thought your father was only considering selling," I said, glancing up at Brad.

"Me, too. What would a construction worker want with an already built building?" He slipped the card into his pocket. "The questions keep piling up without any answers."

"They'll come."

We continued weaving our way through the crowd, receiving some ominous looks and some curious ones. I guessed a lot of people were waiting to see what Brad intended to do with his father's holdings.

"Okay, your father has...had...the strip mall and the apartment complex. Word is, he thought about selling the complex. What else did he own around here others might be interested in?"

Brad led me to a pair of padded wicker chairs and lowered into one. "I thought those were it, but now I'm not sure. No one seems concerned about the mall, do they? There has to be something else he was working on. With what funds, though? Building that complex pretty much drained his finances."

I sat in the other chair, putting my hand on his arm. "We'll figure it out."

"Are you always this optimistic?"

"I try to be." If not, I'd grumble myself into a self-pitying pile. "You need to get your father's laptop back."

"I'm hoping he made a backup and hid the drive somewhere."

"A safety deposit box?"

His face brightened. "Now, you're talking. I'm sure I'll find a key somewhere in his apartment if he had one. Want to come help me look? It isn't that late yet."

Although we'd already searched the penthouse, now we had something in particular to look for. "Sure." I couldn't wait to kick off my secondhand shoes no matter how cute they were.

We waited outside for the valet to bring Brad's car. After twenty minutes, a harried young man in a red jacket sprinted our way. "I'm sorry, sir. We've misplaced the keys. Please, have a seat inside while we search for them. I'm sure they're on the wrong hook."

Brad's brows lowered. "Are you saying someone may have stolen my car?"

"No, no…" he held up his hands. "I'll find them." He turned and darted away.

"That's just great." Brad led me back inside to a leather sofa in the main room. "Things have been against me from the moment I stepped foot in this town."

"Why would someone steal your car?"

"To slow us down?" He shook his head. "Maybe we're closer than we think to finding the killer, although I don't have a clue who it might be."

I sat against the back of the sofa and toed off my shoes. "We've only spoken with Roberts and Jenkins, and only in passing. I can't see where anyone would consider us much of a threat at this point."

He laid his head back and closed his eyes. "I'm so tired. I want time to grieve and settle my dad's affairs. Is that too much to ask?"

Not knowing what to say, I simply sat there and held his hand.

The club manager arrived a few minutes later with complimentary champagne. "I'm so sorry, Mr. Armstrong. I promise you this type of thing never happens here."

"It's the way things have been going lately." Brad handed me a flute and took one for himself.

I normally didn't drink, but tonight certainly warranted something to settle my nerves. I sipped the drink. This wasn't the cheap stuff I'd had at a wedding before. Smooth and bubbly. I took another sip and felt the butterflies in my stomach start to settle.

"Sorry for the foul mood," Brad said, draining his glass. "I shouldn't take my frustrations out on you."

This was taking his frustrations out on me? Sighing and resting his head against the chair had to be the mildest form of aggression I'd ever seen.

"Found your car, sir." The valet rushed to our side. "That's the good news."

Brad groaned. "What's the bad news?"

"It's, uh, half submerged in the pond."

"What?" Brad bolted to his feet.

"Seems someone took the car for a joy ride. It's a really nice car." The young man took a step back. "It wasn't me, though."

"Who was it?" Brad leaned closer, growling.

"I don't know, but I've called a tow truck."

"Good. Now call for a car to pick us up. I hope this place has good insurance."

"The…the…best," the manager stammered. "The absolute best."

I glanced past him into Roberts' snide face. I'd bet my pearls he had something to do with this. I stood, more than ready to leave.

Just then I caught a whiff of the infamous cologne and whirled in time to see a man in a suit hurrying out the front door. "Brad?"

"I smell it." He grabbed my hand, and we dashed outside.

The man climbed into a medium-sized sedan and sped away.

Chapter 10

The next morning I stared woefully at the front door, willing Brad to enter with coffee. After half an hour, I sighed and headed to my apartment to make my own. I returned a little later with three cups and still no Brad.

"Why the long face?" Shar glanced over from where she hung a new shipment of leashes. Despite the fact she wasn't officially supposed to start work until the next week, the woman made her own hours, and I was too tired to argue.

"Brad didn't bring my coffee."

"Aren't we a spoiled little girl. Did the two of you fight last night?"

"No." I told her about someone taking his car and it ending up in the pond.

"There you have it. He's most likely waiting to rent one. They don't open until nine. Want me to open yesterday's mail? Oh, and I found a note in the door when I arrived this morning."

"Sure, go ahead." I booted up my computer to

check pet boarding reservations. I really wanted to talk to Heather about the conversation with her husband last night, but she'd called and said she'd be in late this morning.

"What's this?" Shar dropped a sheet of copy paper on the counter in front of me. "What have you gotten yourself into?"

I glanced down to see the words STOP NOSING AROUND in big black letters. I swallowed against a suddenly dry throat. "I'm helping Brad find out who killed his father."

Shar leaned on the counter across from me. "I'll help. I read every Nancy Drew and Trixie Belden book ever written." She tapped her forefinger against her temple. "I can sniff out a clue better than a bloodhound."

"Considering I've just received a threat, you should probably not get involved." Maybe the taking of Brad's car hadn't been a simple joy ride but a warning.

"You cannot bow down to threats. Tell me what you know."

I studied her eager face. Could I trust this woman I hardly knew? Maybe. She did seem to know a lot of people in Waterfall. Starting with finding Mr. Armstrong dead, I told her all that we'd learned.

Her gaze never left my face as I talked. When I'd finished, she nodded. "I say you take that cat everywhere you go. When he gets agitated by someone, you confront that person."

"That could get me killed." I drew back.

"Maybe, but then maybe not. Go on the offense

is what I always say." She slapped the counter. "Someone thinks you know something. Act as if you do and keep them on their toes. I can see you need my help. I'll volunteer my time here in the store on my days off. Together we'll catch this guy!" She raised a fist in victory.

I shook my head at her enthusiasm. "I prefer a more…modest approach. Find some clues and turn them over to the authorities."

"And lose out on the glory?" She frowned.

"Better that than dead."

She rolled her eyes and grabbed a broom from the closet. "I'm going to sweep the sidewalk out front and clear my head." She exited as Mrs. Nelson entered with Greta.

"Is that the new groomer?" Mrs. Nelson set the pet carrier on the floor. "Where are the cats?"

"I kept them in the apartment today. They try more and more each day to slip out the door when someone enters. Yes, that's Shar, the new groomer." I bent and baby-talked with the dog.

"Wonderful. I have a list of requirements in my purse I'd like to give her." She turned and stepped outside.

I watched as she handed a paper to Shar who glanced at it and nodded, then said something that caused Mrs. Nelson to frown. They seemed to banter back and forth a while until Mrs. Nelson marched away, head high, and Shar came back inside.

"What was that all about?" I asked.

"She wants a Schnauzer to have a Yorkie cut. How ridiculous is that? I refused, of course, but promised she'd be well pleased with the cut I give her dog on Tuesday."

"Maybe you should have given her what she wanted and let her see what a bad idea it was."

"And waste my time? No thank you." She opened the door to the carrier and scooped out Greta, putting her in the large play area on one side of the store.

"She doesn't like the dog to have a lot of playtime."

"Oh, pooh. What she doesn't know won't hurt her, will it, sweetie?" She ruffled the dog's ears.

I started to remind her that I was the boss, and customer service was key when Brad opened the door to let Heather in, then followed. "You're earlier than I thought."

"Bobby is home with the baby. No need for me to be there, too." She ducked her head but not before I saw her red eyes.

"Is everything okay?"

"No. Bobby was fired from his mechanics job. All we have now are the odd jobs he'll get from Mr. Roberts." She slumped into the desk chair behind the counter. "I don't think my marriage will survive this."

"Sure, it will."

She shook her head. "He's lied to me too many times. I think he might be doing something illegal."

I glanced up to meet Brad's interested gaze, before returning my attention to Heather. "Like what?"

"Have you been reading the paper?" Her brows rose. "A lot of stolen cars happening around town

CAT-EYED WITNESS

and a lot of similar ones being sold by Roberts Auto. What if Bobby is helping make the cars hard to distinguish between the stolen ones and the ones being sold?"

That was a definite possibility. If Brad's car hadn't ended up in the pond, it might have been resold. "Where's your car, Brad?"

"Roberts Auto. It's the only repair place in town. I doubt they'll steal it from their own lot."

"No, but it does give you a reason to do some snooping around over there." I grinned.

"That it does. See you tonight at the meeting." He smiled and left, turning at the door. "I won't forget your coffee in the morning."

"See that you don't." I chuckled. "I'm not a morning person."

"That's putting it mildly," Shar said.

With a laugh, he left, leaving me to my work and long overdue emails and billing. While I loved my job, I had a strong desire to snoop around the auto repair shop with him. I had a feeling I'd want to do almost anything with him.

"I'm not needed now that Heather is here. See you tonight." Shar grabbed her oversized purse from under the counter and sailed from the store.

"Does she make you as tired as she does me?" Heather asked.

"Yep. Now, she insists on helping me and Brad."

"Extra eyes and a different way of seeing things might not be a bad idea. You know I'd be right with you if I didn't have a child."

"I know. It would be like old times, getting into

trouble in high school." Sometimes, being an adult lacked the fun factor. At least until Brad arrived in town. "Isn't it strange how quickly folks changed their minds about Brad once he decided to renovate rather than raise rents?"

"Not really." She shrugged. "People are fickle around here. Do what they want and they love you; otherwise you're regarded with suspicion." She propped her chin in her hand. "What am I going to do about Bobby?"

"Maybe Brad can find out something. He knows a lot of businessmen. Perhaps he can look into whether Bobby's actually doing something illegal. What if he is?"

"It's the nail in the coffin." Tears welled in my eyes. "I haven't said anything, but we've been having trouble since Robbie was born."

"I'm sorry." I put my hand on her shoulder. "We'll figure this out, just like we always do."

She sniffed and nodded. "I'm not sure I'm cut out to be a single mom, though."

"Stop thinking that way. We don't know anything yet." I handed her the warning note in hopes of diverting her attention away from her troubles. "I received this today."

Her eyes widened. "Trinity! You could be in danger."

"Exciting, huh?" Not really, but it worked in switching her train of thought. I went on to tell her of what we'd found out last night, minus the conversation with her husband.

"Someone stole Brad's car and drove it into the pond? That's why it's in the shop?"

80

"Seems that way."

"Bobby owes me big time. Want me to ask him if he knows anything about it? I'm pretty sure he'd tell me. He needs to score some points before I kick his rear to the curb." And just like that we were back to her marriage. "In fact, I'll call him right now."

"You don't think he'll tip off someone?"

"Not if he wants to live to see another day." She dug her cell phone out of her purse. "It's me. I have a question for you to answer, and don't even think about lying. Do you know anything about the Mercedes that ended up in the country club pond? Uh huh. Are you sure? Really? Okay, pack your bags and bring Robbie here." She hung up. "Bobby took the car. Not as part of the car-stealing ring but because his car was blocked in and he left the club in anger. Said he almost hit a duck and swerved. I'm getting a separation. I. Cannot. Do. This."

At least we knew what happened to the Mercedes. "I'll let Brad know. It won't be good for Bobby."

"At this point, I don't care." She stood and stormed from the front of the store.

That mystery was easily solved. Too bad Mr. Armstrong's murder couldn't be as simple. Wait a minute. Heather hadn't mentioned a car thief ring in her phone call. Why would Bobby mention one if he weren't involved? Things looked darker and darker for my friend.

I returned to work on the computer, leaving arriving doggie and kitty daycare arrivals to Heather, only stopping when she handed me another typed note. This one said, "Strike Two."

"What does that mean?" I hadn't even left the store.

Her face darkened. "Either my husband ratted out my phone call or his phone is tapped."

Wow. "How do we fix that?"

"I don't call him."

"But…if you talk to him at home, I'm willing to bet your house is bugged, too." I called Brad. "Do you know anyone that can see if a house is bugged? I'm not talking about the four or eight-legged kind either."

"I have someone. Whose house?"

"Heather's." I told him of her phone call with Bobby.

"At least I know what happened to my car. I do want to talk to her husband before deciding whether to press charges. How about the two of you meet me at her house when you close up for the day."

"The meeting, remember?"

"Right. Okay. After the meeting. I'm not learning anything here. Roberts hasn't shown up, and his mechanics don't seem to know anything. Let's concentrate our efforts on persuading Bobby to talk, then decide our next move."

"Sounds like a plan." I hung up and told Heather what we'd decided. "Are you really okay with this? We might find out that Bobby is really in deep."

She hiked her chin. "I'd rather know than not. If he's guilty, he needs to pay the price for his choices."

I sure didn't want to be her husband if he was involved. My mild-mannered friend sometimes had sharp teeth.

Chapter 11

Still determined to prove Moses could identify the killer, I struggled with the cat, finally maneuvering him into his carrier in preparation for the evening's mall meeting. He'd howl about being cooped up, but the noise I'd heard come from his little mouth when I'd found Mr. Armstrong was completely different.

"Now you're thinking." Shar grinned from the front door. "Let the sniffing begin."

"I wasn't expecting you to attend the meeting." I lifted the carrier.

"Why not? I work here. Whatever is planned will affect me, too. Besides, you need my help solving this mystery." She rubbed her hands together. "Remember, I'm well-read."

The more the merrier, they say. I stepped outside and locked the store behind us. Besides, Brad had asked me to arrive early to help set up. Shar would come in handy. I eyed the bag she carried. "What's that?"

"Finger foods. People are happier with something to munch on. I've got a veggie tray, a fruit tray, and ham and cheese sliders. Will there be tea?"

I shrugged. "I'm not sure anyone thought that far ahead."

I was wrong. Brad had catered the event with fancy foods.

Shar frowned and slid her bag under the table. A flicker of defeat crossed her face.

"No, ma'am," I said. "You set out what you brought. Folks around here like simpler fare."

"Are you sure?"

"Absolutely." I set Moses's carrier in a seat in the front row, then thought better of it and placed him in the back. This way, he'd get a whiff of everyone who entered. The cat gave a sad meow as I walked away, tugging at my heart strings. He'd be okay. I'd be next to him in a few minutes.

Brad stared at Shar. "Did I do something wrong by having food catered?"

"No, she shouldn't have assumed. Now, we'll have a variety." Other than stuffed mushrooms, crackers with what I strongly suspected was caviar, and a chocolate fountain surrounded by fruit, my guess was that Shar's offering would go much faster.

"I have a lot to learn." He unfolded a chair, setting it in place. When we'd finished, we had five rows of five with extra chairs leaned against the wall. How many people did he expect with only six residents?

He must have deciphered the confusion on my

face. "I have a few people coming who are interested in the vacant storefronts."

"Maybe you'll sign a lease tonight."

He chuckled. "It rarely happens that fast, but I'm hopeful for the near future. I've already hired an architect to draw up plans for the theater. He's supposed to bring them tonight so I can get moving on finding a contractor."

"What about the other store?"

"At first, I'd thought about a dollar store, but that would affect the thrift store. So I have a guy coming who's interested in a small organic food store."

I raised my eyebrows, not sure how popular that would be in a small town where people loved their fried food. But, since I didn't have a better idea, I kept my mouth shut and returned to the back row where I sat next to Moses.

A few minutes later, people started trickling in. Most of them I knew from the mall, but a few were strangers. They were the ones who took the seats in the front row.

Moses howled as two men in slacks and button-up shirts passed us by. A scent trail of the infamous cologne trailed behind one of them. Aha. It was strangers who raised the cat's hair. I'd be keeping an eye on them.

The door opened behind me as Brad stood in front of a makeshift podium. I turned to see Mr. Roberts and another man enter. Instead of sitting, they stood against the back wall as if they wanted to dart out as soon as possible. What purpose did a used car salesman have at this meeting?

"I asked all of you to email me concerns about improving your rental properties," Brad said. "We'll start with those, then move on to the two vacant properties." He flipped through a note pad in front of him. "Tail-Waggin' doesn't seem to have any issues that need addressing." He smiled in my direction. "The hardware store would like to be painted, as do all the others. We plan on painting inside and out." He continued stating every concern before turning to the vacant properties.

"We have with us today a few businessmen interested in the property in which we're holding this meeting. The other property is moving forward as a movie theater, which I will own rather than rent. Each person interested in the property we all sit in will approach the podium and give their pitch. Then we'll cast a vote."

The room exploded into applause.

"I didn't know he'd handle this so democratically," Shar whispered. "You should hold onto that man, in my opinion. He's made from good stock."

"Shh." For goodness sake. I didn't plan on holding on to anyone.

The first man to take the podium after Brad stepped to the side was Mr. Roberts. He swaggered to the front as if he already did business there and gripped the microphone. "What better use of this space than a used car showroom? Imagine a line of fine automobiles lined up outside with the cream of the crop displayed behind large glass windows?"

The room erupted with a chorus of no's and no way's. I agreed. We didn't need our parking lot filled with cars for sale. It would definitely make parking more difficult for our customers.

Mr. Roberts raised his hands. The room scttlcd down. "Now, hear me out. Folks from all around would come to purchase a car and take notice of your places of business. This is something that would benefit us all."

"What's he up to?" Shar leaned close. "That's the dumbest thing I've ever heard. Have you seen the size of his car lot? Why, he'll take over the place."

"Maybe that's his plan." I kept my attention glued to the front of the room.

When Mr. Roberts finished, one of the strangers took his place. "I'm Hank Stevenson. I'd like to rent this space as an organic food market. Today, people want to eat healthier, exercise more, and take better care of themselves. Imagine the finest produce, the freshest meats, vitamins and, non-gluten food. Thank you."

The man who had entered with Mr. Stevenson now stood in front of us. "I'm Joe Evans, and I'd like to turn this fine space into a modern workout gym with water massage, yoga classes, and fully equipped showers. Everything a gym goer could ask for." Applause erupted.

I had no doubt which way people would vote. A gym sounded nice, actually—a good way to unwind after a busy day at work.

When the people interested in the space were finished, Brad encouraged us to mingle and to enjoy the food provided, dropping our vote in the box provided near the door. Perfect. I stood and grasped the handle of Moses's carrier. I'd move around the room, listening for his telltale howl and hiss.

"What are you doing with the cat?" Brad popped a cracker covered with caviar into his mouth.

"Paying attention to how he acts around the people here."

A small fish egg rested on his lip. His tongue flicked out to capture it before he smiled down at me. "Want something to eat?"

"Not that. It's like eating salty eyeballs."

His laughter rang out above the many conversations in the room. "You honestly think that cat will lead us to the killer?"

"Yes, I do."

"Okay. I'll play along."

"What's the name of the cologne you sometimes wear?"

"You've asked before. It's Infamous. It's a very popular scent."

"No, really. What's the name?"

"That's the name. Strange how fitting it is, isn't it?'

"Weird." Moses started fidgeting in his carrier as we approached Evans and Stevenson. When we moved closer, I could tell it was Evans that wore Infamous. Moses hissed and growled.

Had we found the killer this easily? I plastered on a smile and tightened my grip on the careening carrier.

Both men stared at the carrier. "That cat does not seem friendly," Evans said.

"He's actually quite the sweetheart, but he's

traumatized because he witnessed the murder of his owner."

Brad elbowed me. "Gentlemen, it's nice you could make our meeting."

Evans dragged his gaze around from Moses. "Never miss an opportunity for expansion. If these fine people vote for me, I'll carry some of Mr. Stevenson's energy drinks, so we'll both benefit."

"Did you know Mr. Armstrong's father?" I asked, drawing the conversation back to where I wanted it to be.

"Of course." He seemed taken aback.

"Did you have business dealings with him?"

Brad nudged my foot. "Excuse Miss Ashford. She tends to be overly curious about some things."

What was wrong with him? I thought we were here to work.

"I'd spoken to Mr. Armstrong about this very space before his death," Evans said. "We had tentative plans before he started talking about selling."

"He was going to sell the mall?" Brad stiffened.

"He'd mentioned it, along with the apartment complex. Nothing ever came of our conversation. Until you brought it back to light, I'd decided to turn my attentions elsewhere. I'm glad to know the property is still available for lease."

Mr. Armstrong had a lot of secrets.

"Slider?" Shar held out a tray of ham and cheese encased in tiny buns.

Mr. Roberts joined us, snatching two sliders from the tray. "I cannot believe my idea was so soundly turned down by these petty people."

A muscle ticked in Brad's jaw. "They're entitled to decide who joins their ranks. I can't afford to lose tenants."

The man bit a slider in half. "Right. Your father got himself into a bit of trouble. I've heard he owns several people money."

"Would you be one of them?" I asked. Things were starting to get interesting.

"You're a nosy little thing, aren't you?" Roberts gave an indulgent laugh. "Remember what happened to the curious cat." Still laughing, he left, sauntering through the open front door.

"Excuse us." I pulled Brad away from the other two men. "I know your father had financial problems, but did you know he owed people?"

"No. This complicates things. We need to find out who he owed and how much."

"How do we do that?" My fingers had grown numb trying to hold onto the cat carrier, so I set it at my feet and flexed my hand.

"I need my father's laptop." He sighed. "I either have to find a backup drive or convince McIlroy to return the laptop to me."

"Looks like we'll be busy. Not only do we need to search the apartment more thoroughly, but we need to talk to Bobby Langley." And make a suspect list that continued to grow. "Did you see how Moses reacted to Evans? I bet he's our killer."

"Like I told you, Infamous is a popular cologne. I bet half the people my father did business with wore the same scent. Leave the cat out of this."

I would not, but I would take the cat on some investigating of my own. I'd find the next big event happening among the area's businessmen and find a way in. One of these suits killed Brad's father, and Moses knew which one.

I'd bet my life on it.

Chapter 12

The dog grooming business was booming, and Shar quickly moved to three days a week. As renovations started around the Waterfall mall, the town's interest turned on us. I'd been so busy I still hadn't had a chance to talk to Bobby or see much of Brad.

Not to mention how moody my friend had become. I watched as a serious-faced Heather handed a sippy cup to Robbie who played in the dog pen with a couple of fuzzy poodle puppies someone had dropped off for me to sell. Seems not only was Tail-Waggin' a daycare and grooming business, but now a pet consignment store. Weird. Why not sell the puppies yourself rather than split the proceeds?

When Heather emitted another exasperated sigh, I said, "Okay. What's up? If your face fell any further, you'd be stepping on your bottom lip."

She stepped away from her son and leaned on the counter. "Bobby didn't come home last night."

"Did you have a fight?"

She nodded. "I brought up our financial woes and his untruths. He told me I didn't know what I was talking about and that things could get worse before they got better." Tears welled in her eyes. "I'm scared, Trinity."

I put my hand on her arm. "What started the fight?"

"I found a wad of hundred-dollar bills in his jacket pocket and got suspicious. Asked for some of it to pay bills. He told me the money wasn't his and every cent was accounted for. There's no doubt in my mind now that he's doing something illegal."

Considering he'd stolen Brad's car, we already knew he was up to no good. I guessed my friend hadn't wanted to accept her hubby's wrongdoings. "Where do you think he went?"

She shrugged. "I'm so mad at him I could spit, but I also don't want anything to happen to him. He is the father of my child. I should get to work and take my mind off things." She moved to a pile of unpacked boxes, glancing occasionally to where her child giggled and rolled around with the puppies.

Although I'd miss the little furballs, I did need to put an ad in the paper. I eyed the store with new eyes. One wall with no windows could easily support glass enclosures for pets to be sold. I'd have to be creative with the other products, but it might work.

Trashcan and Sharkbait raced to the front window, chubby Moses on their tails. All three sat and stared across the parking lot to where construction had begun on the new theater. Brad headed across the lot toward Tail-Waggin'.

Silly how happy I felt seeing him coming my way. "Hello, stranger," I said as he entered.

He bent and shooed the cats away from the door. "I'm sorry. The renovations here have taken up more of my time than I thought." He straightened and grinned. "But, I did find something interesting in my father's mattress."

"Do tell." I folded my arms on the counter, my eyes soaking up the face I'd been missing.

He pulled a Jumpdrive from his pocket and put it on the counter. "Want to take a look at this tonight? The police still haven't released my dad's laptop, so we'll have to use yours. Mine decided to crash on me."

"After you put the drive in?"

He laughed. "No. Before. Yours should be safe. I'll bring a pizza around six?"

"Sounds perfect." Although I'd like to have searched with him for this treasure, I'd still enjoy the evening with him.

"Pipe's busted! Room's flooded." Shar dashed past us carrying a fifty-pound mixed breed dog, dripping water everywhere. "Need help getting the animals out." She headed through the back door to where the kennels were.

Brad and I exchanged a glance before racing to the grooming station. If I'd been paying attention to the store instead of him, I'd have seen through the glass that water sprayed from around the pipe in the wall where the hose connected.

"Where's the shutoff to the water?" Brad asked as I scooped a shih tzu into my arms.

"Behind the bathtub." Leaving him to deal with

the geyser, I carried my rescue to the kennels and wondered how the owners would take knowing their pups weren't groomed.

"Crisis averted for now." Brad came up behind me and handed me a towel. "Just needed tightening, but you might want to contact a plumber to check things out."

"Can we use the water?"

He nodded. "I think so."

"Back to work for me, then. I thought we were all going to drown." Shar carried the dog in her arms back to the grooming area.

A bit of an exaggeration, but nothing was boring with Shar around. I turned to the stack of mail on the counter and opened a white envelope with only my name written across the front. Not too suspicious under normal circumstances. Several of the customers would pay by slipping an envelope with payment through the mail slot. But, considering I'd already received one warning, my fingers shook as I pulled out a sheet of folded paper.

"Stop asking questions," I read out loud.

"What?" Brad whipped around at my voice, one hand on the doorknob.

"Another warning." The only place I'd recently asked questions was the mall meeting, and that had been days ago.

"Put that down and call McIlroy," Brad said. "No more fingerprints."

"Oh, right." Idiot. I should have known not to touch it, but if I hadn't taken it out of the envelope, I wouldn't have known what it said. I dropped the paper and picked up the phone. The police receptionist said someone would be by shortly.

"Do you want me to stay?" Concern crossed Brad's face.

"No. You're busy. I'm not going anywhere today. Not with my workload, and the police will be by. I'm perfectly safe."

"I'm a phone call away." With one last, lingering glance, he left the store.

"I don't like this," Heather said. "Two warning notes since Brad arrived."

"It isn't his fault. I'm the one being outright nosy." I glanced through the rest of the mail, separating bills from junk, not glancing up until the bell over the door jingled and Detective McIlroy entered.

He glanced at Heather before standing in front of me. "You received a threatening note?"

"Yes, the second one. Sorry, but I don't know where the first one is."

"Top right drawer." Heather lifted her son from the pen. "I'm taking my lunch, so the two of you can talk." She headed to the back of the store.

I dug out the first note and handed it to McIlroy. "Guess this will have my friend's fingerprints, too. The second note only mine."

He read both notes and, wearing a pair of gloves, slipped them into an evidence bag. "What have you gotten yourself into?"

"What you told me. I'm trying to clear my name and find out who killed Mr. Armstrong."

"Who have you been questioning?"

"Everyone who knew him, and everyone who wears the cologne Infamous." I crossed my arms.

"Just simple questions like what their business with him was." I went on to tell him of Moses's reaction to Evans' and Bobby's confession of driving Brad's car into the clubhouse pond.

His brow lowered. "Why didn't you tell me about Mr. Langley's confession immediately?"

"Because I don't want you putting him in jail until I can speak with him further."

"Haven't you heard of visiting hours?" He shook his head. "I'll need to speak to the man."

"He's MIA."

"You know this how?"

I jerked my head toward the back of the store. "His wife is my friend and she told me."

"Why are you making me pull every bit of information from you bit by bit? Please call your friend out here."

"Heather!" I smiled as McIlroy's head jerked. "Could you come out here, please?"

She poked her head around the corner. "I'm on my lunch." Her gaze on the detective showed her reluctance.

"I'd like to speak with you regarding your husband, Mrs. Langley."

She tossed her ponytail over her shoulder and sulked toward him, practically dragging poor Robbie who held half a peanut butter and jelly sandwich in his free hand. "I don't know where he is. He left last night in a hissy fit and hasn't called."

McIlroy drew air through his nose slowly. "If you hear from him, I have some questions." He returned his attention to me. "As for you, clearing your name shouldn't mean meddling in the business of dangerous people."

I blinked like an owl subjected to sudden light. "How else will I find out anything? Isn't that how the police do it? Ask questions?"

"You aren't the police. It's best you search through Mr. Armstrong's finances and business records and see whom he owed money to and who might have wanted him out of the picture. Behind-the-scenes kind of stuff."

"You can do those things yourself."

He actually groaned. "Some things are missing off his laptop, Miss Ashford. I'm asking for your cooperation."

Asking must have hurt. I grinned. "I'll do my best."

"Be careful." With that, he turned and strode from the store.

"Why did you tell him about Bobby?" Heather's face reddened. "Don't I have enough to deal with?"

"I'm sorry, but he asked, and I don't want to go to jail for withholding information pertinent to an investigation."

Her shoulders sagged. "I'm out of my element."

"But you aren't alone." I moved to her side and wrapped her in a hug.

"What's going on?" Shar stepped in and added her arms to the hug fest. "I love a good hug."

"My husband didn't come home last night," Heather muttered.

"Another woman?" Shar asked.

"That would be the best of possibilities." She sniffed.

Shar stepped back and studied her for a second,

then nodded. "You come sit down and fill me in. I've heard through the grapevine your man is in some trouble. Between the three of us girls, we'll get things straightened out in no time. I guarantee it."

Since the store was empty at the time and Robbie was busy letting puppies lick the remnants of his sandwich off his fingers, we gathered around the counter. Shar darted away and returned with two chairs from the back.

"I'm all ears. Want me to lock the front door?"

"We're open for business, Shar." I frowned.

"Some things are more important." She plopped into a chair. "Tell me everything, Heather."

My friend glanced to where Robbie played and lowered her voice, telling Shar of her money problems, Bobby stealing Brad's car, and their fight the night before. "I know he's doing something wrong."

"Then, we need to find him and put a stop to his shenanigans. He'll have a price to pay, but your worries will be eased. All in?" She held her hand out.

I glanced at Heather who put her hand over Shar's. I sighed and put my hand over hers. Just great. Not only was I helping Brad clear our names, but now I had to find a wayward husband who most likely didn't want to be found and might be in more danger than we could handle.

What could possibly go wrong?

Chapter 13

After staying late making a list of possible places Bobby might be hiding, I barely made it upstairs to change before Brad arrived. I smelled the pizza through the closed door and yanked it open. "Hello. I'm starving."

Brad laughed. "Glad to see you, too." He brushed past me and set the pizza in the center of the table. "Want to eat and look at the drive or eat first?"

Shrugging, I opened the box. Yum, lots of pepperoni and sausage. "Whichever, as long as we don't get grease on my keyboard."

"We can wait." He grabbed a slice of pizza and sat in a kitchen chair. "How was your afternoon? Talk to McIlroy?"

With my own slice in hand, I sat across from him. "Yes, and there is something off about his investigation. He told me to clear my name without asking questions, and that I should be more focused on files missing from your father's computer." I raised my brows. "He wants us to find and turn over what he can't. Your father removed something, and McIlroy wants to know what. That seems to be his primary focus."

"Maybe he thinks that will lead to the killer." Brad reached for another slice of pizza. "It might, you know." He wiped his fingers on a napkin. "I'm itching to take a look at that Jumpdrive."

I slid my laptop over to him, hoping we'd find something useful. Grabbing a pad of paper and a pencil from a kitchen drawer, I sat next to Brad, ready to make a list of suspects.

"Password?" Brad's fingers poised over the keys.

"Dogs123."

"Cute." He laughed and typed, then inserted the drive. "Here's hoping."

I leaned over as several files appeared. Bingo. Financial records for Armstrong Inc. "What's that one?" I pointed to one labeled Business Dealings. If it was what I thought it was, Mr. Armstrong wasn't doing a very good job of hiding anything.

"This is too easy," Brad said as names appeared. "Nothing seems suspicious. If Dad had dirt on someone, it would be in a misleading file." He tucked his tongue in his cheek and leaned closer to the screen.

After a few minutes, he pulled up the trashcan and browsed the deleted files there. "Clever. See here? He labeled this file Brad's achievements. Dad wanted me to find this."

"That meant mean he suspected someone wanted to kill him." My blood froze.

"It's starting to look that way." He opened the

file. Names with typed notes came up.

"This is definitely what McIlroy is looking for." I couldn't believe the abundance óf information. "Look. He's tagged Roberts with suspicions of car theft, and Harold Jenkins with embezzlement." I didn't see proof, though.

"It appears both men came to my father hoping to form a partnership of some kind. When that didn't work, Evans offered to purchase not only the mall, but the apartment complex. Dad turned them both down."

The mall would make a spectacular used car lot. I was glad the other residents had turned Roberts down. "Now what? Do we turn this over to McIlroy?"

"I'm not sure." He straightened in his chair. "I'd like to investigate further. Let it leak out that I might be considering selling the complex. See whether anyone takes the bait."

"Be careful. I'm going to help Heather find her runaway husband. If we do, we can ask him what he knows. Do you think McIlroy will provide police protection if he comes forward?"

"I don't see why not." He ejected the drive and slipped it into his pocket. "I saved the files on your laptop under pet supplies if you want to do some digging. I'm beat." He pushed to his feet.

I followed him to the door. "See you tomorrow."

Brad smiled. "Thank you for your help." He placed a quick, impulsive kiss on my cheek.

Stunned, I put a hand to my face as he strolled out the door. Sleep was a long time coming that night as I dreamed of what it would be like to feel Brad's lips on mine.

Usually, Sunday mornings provided time for me to sleep in since the shop was closed. Not today. Shar and Heather, minus Robbie, waited on the sidewalk.

"Where's the baby? Did Bobby come home?" Dumb question. My friend would have called off the search if her husband was watching his son.

"I talked my neighbor into watching him. I hated to, because they work five days a week, but I promised we'd only be a couple of hours." Heather handed me a mocha-flavored iced coffee.

Shar narrowed her eyes. "You look different this morning. Happier than usual."

"I slept well."

"No, you didn't. You have bags under your eyes." She crossed her arms.

"Yeah." Heather stared at me. "What secret dwells behind those brown eyes?"

Was I really that transparent? "Fine. Brad kissed me on the cheek when he left last night. It didn't mean anything. One friend to another." I brought the coffee to my lips.

"Then why is your hand trembling?" Shar asked too many questions.

"Can we get busy on the reason I'm not still in bed sleeping?" I glared over the rim of my cup. "Where to first?"

"Roberts Automotive," Heather said. "They're closed on Sunday. Maybe Bobby is sleeping in the office or the garage."

I doubted it, but at least it was a starting place. "Who's driving?"

"Me." Shar dangled car keys in front of me. "It's the Thunderbird today. I only drive it on Sundays." She led us to a dream of a car. A teal 1957 Thunderbird convertible in mint condition.

"This is even more beautiful than Brad's leather seats." I ran my hand over the hood.

"No touching. She's freshly waxed." Shar wiggled her finger at me.

I slid into the front seat, leaving the back all to Heather. "What do you drive the rest of the week?" I'd never drive anything else.

"A simple Toyota Tacoma king cab." She sat in the driver's seat and turned the key in the ignition. The engine roared to life. "Ready for an adventure, girls?" Shar laughed and drove from the parking lot, then parked behind Roberts Automotive. "I doubt your husband will respond to a knock on the door, but we can try." The ball of energy exited the car and pocketed her keys before putting a tire boot on. "I'm not taking any chances with my baby. Your hubby already stole one vehicle that we know of."

"Tried to," Heather muttered.

"If he hadn't driven into the pond, he would have succeeded."

Shar flashed a grin. "Let's go catch your hubby."

I laughed and hip bumped my best friend. "She's got you there." We followed Shar to the large showroom windows and peered through cupped hands. There didn't appear to be a single soul moving around, although I did see a Ford

Mustang I'd love to own. Maybe someday.

After rapping on the window and not receiving a reply, Shar led us to the adjacent garage. One bay was empty, and one bay held a car suspended on a steel platform. "Yoo-hoo."

"Bobby?" Heather stood under the car. "If you're there, would you please come down?"

I felt a bit silly talking to an empty vehicle so said nothing, choosing instead to try the handle of a door at the back. The door opened easily at my touch. I turned on the light and stepped inside a small room full of tools and car parts that smelled of gasoline.

I moved to the back of the room. A sleeping bag, a case of bottled water, and bags of jerky and other snacks told me someone was indeed sleeping there. "I think he's been here," I called out.

The other two women rushed to my side. Shar clapped me on the shoulder. "Good sleuthing."

Heather studied the items in front of us. "He does like jerky."

"Who else would be sleeping here?" I frowned. "It has to be him."

"Where is he now?" Shar asked.

Heather's eyes widened. "The diner? He had enough cash on him to be able to eat for quite a few days. Especially if he isn't paying for a hotel room."

"Has anyone but me realized that if Bobby is sleeping here, then Roberts knows?"

"So?" Heather shrugged. "I'm sure my husband said I kicked him out. I didn't, but I was about to."

Something about the situation tickled at my brain. On the surface, it seemed innocent enough, given the circumstances, but it still felt off. I bent and picked up the sleeping bag, sniffing it. "Doesn't smell like anything. Here, you take a whiff." I shoved it at Heather.

She wrinkled her nose but took a deep breath. "I don't smell anything."

"The two of you are silly." Shar yanked the sleeping bag out of her hands and dropped it to the floor. "Neither one of you is a bloodhound. You should have brought that cat." She raised her hand in a forward motion. "To the diner."

I didn't smell Infamous on the bag and I'd never smelled it on Bobby. The cologne was probably out of his price range. Moses wouldn't have been any use in this situation. It wasn't like I could have him sniff the sleeping bag and say, "find Bobby, boy."

A few minutes later, we entered the diner and were led to a corner booth. I craned my neck, trying to spot the man we searched for. "I'll take a diet soda," I said. "I'm going to go to the restroom in a roundabout way and see if I can spot him."

"Nope." Shar stopped me. "I'll do it. He knows you. Show me a picture, sweetie." She pointed at Heather.

Heather pulled a photo from her purse of a happy-looking couple. She sniffed and hiked her chin. "He still looks like this, except with a scowl and a harried expression."

"Got it." Shar slid from the booth. "Tea for me, please." She wove in and out of the tables on her way to the back of the diner.

"She's growing on me," Heather said. "Once I realized her bossiness wasn't personal, I started appreciated her."

To my surprise, I found out I agreed. "She's a hard worker, always willing to lend a helping hand, and full of surprises too." I grinned. "Hiring her has definitely made life more interesting."

"If anyone can find Bobby, it's her."

"Didn't find him," Shar said, sliding back into the booth. "But I didn't check the men's room. Want me to sneak in there?"

I snorted. "Why not ask one of the workers? Our server, for example?" I motioned to a young man in an apron who headed our way.

"Do you know what you want, or do you need a few more minutes?"

"Diet soda, two teas, and for you to go to the restroom and ask if Bobby Langley is in there," Shar said with a grin. "Go to the restroom first." She made a shooing motion with her hands.

The server—Jason, his tag said—stared at her for a moment, then did as he was told. He returned with Bobby in tow.

"Oh, you're going to get such a tip." Shar clapped. "Sit, Mr. Langley. Right there next to your wife. We're ready to order now, and Mr. Langley will pay the bill."

Bobby sputtered. "What are you doing here? Do you realize the danger you've put me in?"

"No, sir." Shar shook her head. "You've done that to yourself."

Heather only glared, scooting as far from him as she could.

I folded my hands on the table and leaned forward. "We understand things are rough for you.

The police are looking for you regarding the attempted theft of Brad's car. We also have learned you've come into a lot of cash lately—"

"I earned it working for Roberts." He crossed his arms. "I'm going to pay off some bills."

"Good." Heather elbowed him. "You need to earn a lot more. Legally, though."

"I'm doing my best."

"Okay, you two. What can you tell us about Roberts and Evans? Their dealings with Mr. Armstrong. Anything to help us find out who killed him." I arched a brow. "You know something. We're going to keep digging until we discover what it is."

He seemed to deflate, sagging into the vinyl. "He has me steal cars, work on them to change their appearance as much as possible, then he resells them."

"How could you do this to us?" Tears sprang to Heather's eyes.

"I gambled away our money. Got desperate. It was the only way to provide for my family."

"Now, you'll go to jail. The police are looking for you."

I tapped on the table. "Do you have proof you can give us before we tell Detective McIlroy where you are?"

He sighed. "I'll turn myself in. As for proof, isn't my word enough? It'll be my word against his, and he has tons of cash to pay for a lawyer, but at least the authorities will have to do some digging."

Bobby pushed to his feet and dropped a hundred-dollar bill on the table. "See you on visiting days, sweetheart."

"We have to find proof that Bobby is telling the truth," Heather said. "Otherwise, he'll take the rap and Roberts will go free."

"Just because Roberts is a thief doesn't mean he's a killer. If he isn't, then the person who killed Mr. Armstrong is still unknown. We need to be very careful."

Chapter 14

Detective McIlroy was waiting outside my apartment when we arrived. "A little bird told me you spent time with Mr. Langley."

Birds traveled fast in a small town. "He's on his way to turn himself in." I grinned, rather proud of what we'd accomplished.

"He hasn't shown up."

Drat. The search was on again. "He was sleeping in the garage of Roberts Auto. Maybe if you question the owner, he'll know where Bobby ran off to."

He glanced at Heather. "Ma'am? Do you know where he might be?"

She chewed a fingernail. "Not really. He doesn't have family. I really thought he'd turn himself in." Her brow furrowed.

Knowing my friend since high school, I could tell something brewed in her mind. I couldn't wait for McIlroy to leave so I could find out what. With a warning to stay safe and not do anything foolish, he headed to his squad car.

I gripped Heather's elbow. "Upstairs and tell me what you're thinking."

"Has anyone noticed how handsome that detective is?" Shar asked. "For a stern man who seems to have no sense of humor, he's nice on the eyes."

Had she grown rabbit ears? "What?"

"How old do you think he is? Fifty? Fifty-five?"

Heather laughed. "Are you falling for him?"

"Maybe. Once we catch this killer. I don't have much of a chance now since we intend to meddle. But later. Not many men can resist this, you know." She waved her hands in front of her, flashed a grin, and then climbed the stairs ahead of us.

"I've barely thought about later today, and she's plotting out a future romance." Heather shook her head. "Guess that's what it's like not to have a husband with a penchant for trouble." She sighed and motioned for me to go ahead of her.

I unlocked the door to my apartment, my mind on what my refrigerator had to offer my friends to drink. "I can make tea."

"Perfect." Shar noticed the notepad I'd left on the table from the night before. "You should hide this. What if your apartment is broken into by the very person you seek?" Sharkbait jumped on the table. "Maybe you need a dog instead of three cats."

I snapped my fingers, the sign for the cat to jump down. "My apartment isn't big enough."

"You might think differently when one of these men come for you." She tapped the notepad. "Did you know they have Women's Night once a month at the Country Club? Did you also know it happens to be tomorrow night?"

"No, but what good will that do us?" I set a pot of water on the stove. "Our suspects are male, and we aren't members."

"I've been a member for years. I just rarely go. The benefit is jilted lovers, dear. I guarantee each of the men in question will have at least one they've tired of at women's night, and bitter women like to talk."

"Single women only, right?" Heather asked. "Which is fine. I can't ask the neighbors to watch Robbie too often."

"We'll make sure to fill you in on whatever we find." Shar flipped to a fresh page in the notepad and started writing names.

"Is there anyone or anything in this town you don't know?" I draped tea bags over cups.

"Nope." She dropped the pen on the table as if dropping a mic. "Five women to look up and make a point of talking to. Wear something nice, Trinity."

"I have the same dress I wore when I went with Brad." I liked the way Shar's mind worked. She definitely had a more intuitive way of thinking than I did. Instead of waiting for a clue to pursue, she went searching for one.

"Well, I don't. Where can I get one in a hurry?"

"The thrift store across the way."

"Then, let that tea steep and let's go."

"I'm going to head home," Heather said. "Since I don't need to go shopping, I'm going to pick up my son. See you at work tomorrow."

She walked out with us and headed for her car

113

while Shar and I crossed to the thrift shop. We arrived just as the doors opened. Since it was Sunday, Mrs. Murdock didn't open until one.

"Good afternoon, ladies." She smiled from the counter. "Where can I point you today?"

"Cocktail dresses. Shar needs one."

"Oh, I see exactly what I want." She made a beeline for a sequined-covered jacket that reminded me of the coat of many colors in the Bible. It had to be the gaudiest thing in the store. "This will go perfect with my red blouse and black skirt. It could even dress up a pair of jeans."

"You'll be noticed for sure." I shielded my eyes as a shaft of sunlight bounced off the jacket and hit me square in the eyes.

"A girl has to make an entrance." She proudly carried the jacket to the counter.

"I've had this jacket for a long time," Mrs. Murdoch said. "I'm so glad it's finally found a home. I'll give you half off. So, twenty-five dollars."

Shar paid and we left. She headed for her car, carefully draping the jacket over the backseat. "You don't think anyone will steal it while we're having tea, do you?"

"Nope." That jacket would be safe hanging from a light post on Main Street.

"Do you have sandwiches to go with the tea?"

"I'm sure I can find something. It'll be nice once the drugstore installs its lunch counter."

"That handsome man of yours is definitely taking his father's dream and running with it."

"He isn't my man, and I didn't think Mr.

Armstrong had any plans for the mall. It never seemed a top priority to him."

"That's where you're wrong. Someone told me that someone told them that Mr. Armstrong wanted to sell the apartments so he could use the money to improve the mall. Too bad it's all hearsay, but it does make sense. Why else would Brad do a 180, and instead of raising rents, start improvements? I guarantee it isn't because of your pretty face. He discovered what his father really wanted to do and, I'd guess, wants to fulfill his last wishes."

What other secrets was Brad keeping from me?

~

Shar picked me up at seven the next evening in the Thunderbird. "Gotta arrive in style. But, I'll tell you this, if anyone tries to steal this baby, I'll shoot them." She patted the black purse on the seat next to her. "I'm always packing."

Oookay? I hated to tell her that the thief was already gone when Brad's car was discovered missing. "You have a permit?"

"Had one for years." She turned the car toward the freeway. "Ready to get nosy?"

With a stern warning to take care of the car or suffer the consequences, Shar handed the keys to the valet. Head high, she sailed into the country club with me on her heels. She paused in the doorway for dramatic effect; at least that's the only reason I could think of for stopping. She did the same thing in the bar, then in the doors leading to the patio which is where a myriad of women in pretty dresses mingled, drinks in their hands.

"Who are we targeting first?" I asked, plucking

a flute of champagne off the tray of a passing server. I wasn't a huge fan but didn't want to draw attention to myself by not having something in hand.

"First, the snack table." Shar made a beeline for a table covered in a white cloth.

Snacks wasn't a grand enough word for the delectable treats set there for our enjoyment. Shrimp, caviar, tiny sandwiches, cookies, and tiny cheesecakes. Why was there a woman's night at the club with no men in sight? Wasn't its purpose for men and women to hook up?

I glanced around the room in case I missed something. Nope. Not a male in sight. "What's the purpose of this monthly gathering?" I whispered to Shar.

"Networking. Some of these women have a lot of power over the men they date. A lot of deals are made through pillow talk." She winked.

Well, that's just gross. "Who here is Roberts' girl?"

"Amelia Turner." Shar popped a shrimp into her mouth. "They broke up a few months ago. She might be willing to spill."

I wasn't a prude or anything, but I did live a rather sheltered life and wasn't crazy about hearing about anyone's intimate details. Please, God, no details.

Amelia was tall, slender, brunette, and might have been beautiful if not for the unapproachable expression on her face. Her hazel eyes narrowed as we approached. "Shar."

"Amy." Shar laughed as high spots of color

appeared on the woman's face. Obviously, she didn't like the shortened version of her name. I spied a bit of dislike between my friend and Amelia and had to admit to some curiosity. There had to be at least twenty years between the two. Would their circles clash that much?

"Nice…jacket." Amelia's lip curled.

"Thank you." Shar ran her hands over the sequins. "I'm pretty sure it's one of a kind."

"I'm sure." Amelia drew air through her nose and turned to me. "You're the new gal on the young Armstrong's arm. Guess that makes you privy to the rest of us."

Not sure what she meant, I shrugged. "Well, uh…Brad and I aren't—"

"Parting anytime soon." Shar stomped on my foot. "Yes, they're the hottest couple in the state right now. Why? Are you interested in him?"

Amelia's gaze roamed over me. "I'm sure I'd come out the victor should I pursue him. What do you want? You wouldn't have spoken to me unless you wanted something."

"I'm simply here to tell you how sorry I am that you and Richard broke up. You have high ambitions and the pickings around this town are rather…slim."

"You aren't his type, Shar."

"I wouldn't touch him with a twenty-foot pole. My eye is on someone else."

"Oh? Care to share?"

"Not a chance."

What twilight zone had I fallen into? Did these women come here to swap stories and find out which rich man was now available? I couldn't imagine anything more pathetic. I'd never been so grateful for my simple life than I was now. The more I looked around the patio area, the more hunger and desperation I saw. My heart ached. My breath caught.

"Excuse me." I made a dash for the ladies room.

Finding an empty stall, I ducked inside and closed the door, leaning against the polished wood. Panic attack. I wasn't in the same boat as those women. Twenty-eight wasn't old-maid material, was it?

Sure, I hadn't gone to veterinarian school, but I did own my own business. That made me a success, right? I didn't need a man to complete me. Feeling better after the small pep talk I'd given myself, I squared my shoulders and exited the stall, joining another woman at the line of sinks.

Chapter 15

It wasn't until I stuck my hands under the faucet that I realized the other woman was crying. I wasn't good with offering solace to strangers and wasn't sure how to handle this situation. Taking my time with soap and water, then grabbing a handful of thick paper towels, I faced her. "Is there something I can do?"

"Not unless you can make Joe Evans love me again." Her answer came barely above a whisper.

"Want to talk about it? You don't know me, but sometimes talking to a complete stranger is the best thing." I tossed the paper towels in the garbage and went to sit on a padded bench, patting the space beside me. "I'm Trinity Ashford."

"Everyone knows who you are. You're the pet store owner who captured the attention of the town's most eligible bachelor."

I felt as if I'd entered the set of *The Bachelor*. Especially with all the women at the club seeming so focused on wealthy men. "We're just friends."

She shrugged. "He doesn't seem interested in anyone else."

"His father was just killed." How could I focus her attention back on Evans? "Why would Mr. Evans dump you? You're gorgeous." The shapely blonde really was stunning. Hazel eyes, full lips, well-endowed in the womanly-curve area. "What's your name?"

"Amber Stirling. Joe said he didn't want to settle down and had grown bored with me. I want marriage and a family. He doesn't."

The jerk. "I'm sorry. Is it because opening the new gym is taking all of his time and focus?"

She snorted, then wiped her eyes with a tissue. "That's just a front. He has his fingers in so many pies I'm surprised they aren't stained purple. He wants the apartment complex, not a space in the mall." Her eyes widened. "Whoops, I shouldn't have told you that. I signed a confidentiality agreement when we started seeing each other."

"Don't worry about it." I might have hit on a gold mine of a clue by coming into the restroom. "He isn't the only one interested in the complex. Why is it so important?"

"It makes a lot of money. Those apartments aren't cheap. I know because I rent one." She stood to leave.

"Who does Joe talk to when he goes there, other than you, of course?"

"The doorman, Mr. Appleton. They seem to be very close."

"What would Mr. Evans do with the complex if he were to obtain it?"

"I've heard him say he'd renovate, raise the rent, and bring in people with greater income. Joe wants to change the town's center from Main Street to the river. He wants to turn Waterfall into a playground for the rich. The mall would be changed to high-scale boutiques and other businesses that cater to the rich." She threw me a sad smile and left.

Shar opened the door and stuck her head in. "You okay? You've been gone a long time."

"Had an interesting conversation with Amber Stirling."

"Wait a minute." Shar checked the other stalls for occupants.

Why hadn't I thought to do that? Just when I thought I might actually be good at this sleuthing thing, I made a rookie mistake. "Did you learn anything?"

She nodded and sat next to me. "Everyone seems to want to own Waterfall."

"Whoa. All I got was that they wanted the apartments."

"Same thing." She pulled a compact from her purse and studied her face, then reapplied lipstick. "We shouldn't stay in here too long. Drinks are flowing, and tongues are loosening. We'll compare notes later. Freshen up."

"Why? Do I need it?"

"Girl, you need to look hungry like the others. Appearances are everything, and those piranhas out there can't understand why Brad wants a tiny thing like you when he could have one of them."

Since I hadn't brought anything but a rose-colored lip gloss, I slathered my lips and patted my hair. It was the best I could do. "Why are they talking about me? We want to know about the men in their lives."

"They'll stop gossiping about you once you're out there. Those women won't say anything to your face." She grinned. "Wouldn't want you to smear their name with handsome Brad."

Good grief. The whole thing was ridiculous. I wanted Waterfall to return to the friendly, small town I always thought it was. I didn't enjoy the dirty little secrets people held, preferring to live in my delusional world where things were cute as puppies and soft as kittens. If only I could sit in my apartment with a plate of buttered biscuits smothered in chocolate gravy and hide from all this.

"Look haughty, not sad," Shar hissed as we stepped back onto the patio. "They think you have something they don't. If it makes you feel any better, Amber used to be an exotic dancer."

It didn't. I spotted Amber in a corner whispering with Amelia. They both turned as Shar and I rejoined the other women. A chilly resentment seemed to have replaced curiosity. "They look as if they want to hurt me."

"They do." She laughed. "See the lovely redhead sitting alone? She's the new mistress of Harold Jenkins, our only married scoundrel."

"Seriously? He's…well…fat. And she doesn't look very old."

"Nineteen, last I heard. Come on, let's join her. She's too young to know how to hold her tongue, and weight doesn't matter if the wallet is fat."

"I need a shower."

"It's all a bit sordid. Welcome to the high life."

"I don't want it." I grabbed a crystal glass of water from a passing server and followed Shar.

"Hello." We sat without being invited. "You seem to be as disliked as the two of us."

"I didn't want to come, but Harold told me to. He said I might learn some things. All I've learned is how to be a snot." She downed the last of the champagne in her flute.

"You're younger than they are. You and Trinity here are the only ones presently attached. Chin up. What's your name?"

"Summer Bassett." She crossed her arms and narrowed her eyes. "I know how this works. You want to know all there is to know about me. Well, here you go. I'm from a dirt-poor farming family in Oklahoma. I met Harold when I waited tables at a greasy diner at a truck stop. He promised to take me away from it all. Well, he did. Now, here I am wearing fine clothes, expensive jewelry, and living alone in a fancy apartment at the whim of an old man. My family hates me. Anything else you want to know?"

I leaned forward. "Does Harold want to buy Waterfall Apartments?"

"Yes."

"Why?"

"He wants to expand to Main Street."

I glanced at Shar. "That would wipe out half the town's small businesses."

She nodded.

"Did he meet with the senior Mr. Armstrong?"

"On multiple occasions."

Confusion clouded my mind. Supposedly, Brad wanted to fulfill his father's last wishes. So, what were they? To sell or to improve? I cut Shar a sideways glance. Who was telling me the truth here? "We should go." I shot to my feet and hurried to the doors, leaving Shar to follow or not.

"That was rude," she said, joining me.

"It won't matter to them." I whirled. "What makes you think Brad's 180 was to fulfill his father's wish, because everything we've learned tonight disputes that."

"Not here." She gripped my arm and waved for the valet to bring the car.

Once we were seated back inside, she put up the roof. "I've lived in Waterfall my whole life. My first husband traveled in the same circles as Armstrong and these other men. I know things. If Brad wanted to raise the rents, he would. He wouldn't be swayed by your pretty face. Something else caused him to change his mind, and I'm guessing it was something his father wanted. That, and he saw that improvements would be as beneficial as higher rents."

"So, you're guessing. You've not actually heard him or anyone else say this." I glared through the dark in the car.

"Let's go ask him right now. You'll see that I'm right." She did a quick U-turn on the Interstate and drove toward Waterfall Apartments.

"It's late, Shar."

"It's best to have your questions answered right now. You need to trust me if I'm going to help you."

I exhaled sharply. I hadn't asked for her help; she'd inserted herself into my investigating and my job. When had I turned into a suspicious person? In the past, I'd always taken a person at face value. Now, I didn't know who to trust. I stared out the passenger window until we parked in front of the apartments.

Mr. Appleton opened the door. "You ladies look quite lovely this evening."

"Been to the club," Shar said, brushing past him. "We're here to see Mr. Armstrong."

"At this hour?" He arched a brow.

She smiled and nodded as she led the way toward the elevator. "Important business."

Wanting to avoid confrontation at all costs, I lagged behind until she gave me an exasperated look as she held the elevator open. "Come on."

"He's going to be asleep."

She rolled her eyes and pressed the button for the penthouse. "It's obvious you'll get no sleep yourself until you have answers."

Most likely true. The doors opened, and we moved forward. I gave a soft knock on Brad's door.

"Good grief, girl." Shar rapped a lot harder.

A few minutes later, a sleepy Brad with mussed hair opened the door. "Trinity?"

I barely managed to rip my gaze from his chiseled chest and the low slung shorts on his hips. "Uh…"

"We have some important things to discuss." Shar pushed her way inside. "Glad to see you're awake."

"I wasn't." He gave me a curious look. "Let me

put on a shirt. Have a seat."

We both perched on the same comfortable sofa I'd sat on many times when visiting with Brad's father. I still couldn't believe he was dead, and that I'd been the one to find his body. Since then, things had moved as fast as a boulder down a steep hill, building momentum until I couldn't get out of the way.

"Okay, what's up?" Brad's gaze landed on me as he sat across from us.

"Why did you change course in regard to the mall? Because it held more benefit than raising rents, or because that's what your father wanted?"

He blinked like an owl in sudden light. "A little of both?"

"Is that a question?" I crossed my arms. "Shar seems to think you've decided to do what your father wanted. Others think you saw the benefit of improvement. Are you aware of the reasons so many people want this complex?"

"I've heard multiple reasons." He relaxed. "I've also decided not to sell. McIlroy released my father's laptop to me. It doesn't have near the information that Jumpdrive does, but it does have his last will and testament. In addition to that, there was a letter to me."

"You made your decision before reading the letter?"

"Yes." His smiled widened. "I saw how much the people of this town meant to my father. Until he built this apartment building, things were simple, life picturesque. I want to do my best to return to his vision as much as possible. Now, where have the two of you been all dolled up?"

I told him what I'd learned at the club. "I don't care if I ever step foot in that place again."

"It's no place for a nice girl like you. I do have to admit that I don't mind those women thinking you're mine. It keeps them off my back."

"For now," Shar said.

"I'll stick to Waterfall and stay away from Silver Brook." Exhaustion weighed on me. "Any idea of the next step in finding out who killed your father?"

His smile faded. "I have a feeling all we can do is wait. Whoever killed him will be coming for me. Whatever grand plans they have, I've ruined them, same as Dad did."

"Who's going to protect you?" My blood chilled.

"I'll have to watch my back with every move I make."

Chapter 16

Shar dropped me off in front of Tail-Waggin'. My steps dragged as I plodded my weary body up the stairs. I stood and stared for a moment at the door. My apartment door had been jimmied open. I dropped my purse on the sofa. "Here, kitties!"

With my heart in my throat, I raced through my apartment in search of three frightened cats. "Here, kitty, kitty." On my way through the kitchen, I grabbed their treats, shaking the can. It never failed to draw them out of hiding.

Not finding them inside, I darted out and down the stairs, shaking the treat can as if my life depended on it. Tears blurred my vision. A meow from under a bush dropped me to my knees. I scooped Trashcan into my arms. "Where are your brothers?" I sprang to my feet and turned in a slow circle before returning to the apartment and putting the cat in the bathroom. Then, I returned downstairs to search for the others, weariness gone and replaced by fear. My cats were my babies. I had to find them.

I located Sharkbait huddling under the dumpster behind the store. No sign of poor Moses, and now rain drizzled from the sky, promising a heavier downpour within minutes. I wouldn't find the other cat on my own.

Back in the apartment, I called Brad, my words breaking with sobs. "Someone...broke in...I can't...find...Moses."

"Hold on." His sleepy voice told me he needed to be more alert. "Let's see if I heard you right. Someone broke into your apartment, the store, what? And Moses is missing? The cat?"

"Yes." I sniffed. "I found the other two, but now it's starting to rain."

"Are you sure no one else is in the apartment?"

"I've searched the whole place." Except for the closet. My gaze shot to the closed door. I had way too many things crammed in there for a person to fit, didn't I?

"I'm on my way. Call McIlroy." Click.

I kicked off my shoes and reached for the closet door. Taking a deep breath, I yanked it open. A shoebox of receipts fell on my head. No one could hide in here. I moved to the walk-in closet in the bedroom and grabbed a high-heeled boot as a weapon. Raising it over my head, I turned on the light, shoving clothes aside to reveal anyone hiding. No one. I quickly changed into shorts and a tee-shirt and called the police.

The receptionist promised to send someone within a few minutes and told me to remain calm.

Easy for her to say. She didn't have a fur baby missing.

Knowing the arriving police officer would want to know if anything other than the cat was missing, I searched the apartment again. My laptop. I thundered downstairs and into the store. My heart rate slowed a bit to see the laptop under the counter where I'd left it. I snatched it up and took it with me as Brad pulled to a stop outside. I motioned through the store window for him to meet me upstairs.

When he did, he immediately pulled me into his arms. "Are you okay?"

"I'm fine," I said, my voice muffled against his wet shirt. "Someone took Moses."

"I'm sure they were looking for something else, and the cat got out. We'll find him. He knows where his food comes from."

The cat could identify Mr. Armstrong's killer. Why couldn't anyone else see that? I pulled free of his embrace and set the laptop on the coffee table. "At least they didn't find this. If I'd left it on the kitchen table as I normally do, they'd have your father's files. Thank you for coming. I didn't know who else to call."

"I'll always come when you ask."

I gazed up at him, reading the warmth in his eyes. Yes, he would drop everything and come. That's the kind of man he was.

His gaze dropped to my lips. He smiled.

I jumped back like a startled rabbit. What was wrong with me? I wanted him to kiss me, didn't I?

The clearing of a throat at the front door pulled me from my thoughts. McIlroy stood there, a grim expression on his face. "Miss Ashford, Mr. Armstrong." He glanced at the door. "What happened here?"

"I arrived home less than an hour ago to this." I waved my arm toward the door. "My cats were gone. I found two, but the cat who can identify the murderer is gone. I think he was taken so he couldn't identify anyone."

McIlroy jerked, then scratched his neck as if he'd stepped in a batch of nettles. "Anything else missing?"

Sighing, I shook my head. "Not that I can tell."

"Why would someone break into your apartment?" He pulled a notepad from his pocket.

"Because I'm nosing around?" Duh. I flopped onto the sofa, listening to my two very unhappy cats in the bathroom meowing their displeasure. "I need to head back out and look for Moses, since no one seems to think he was stolen."

Brad sat next to me, taking my hand in his. "I'll help you look when the detective is finished."

"Mind if I look around?" McIlroy asked.

"Suit yourself."

"I want you to pack a bag and come stay with me in the penthouse," Brad said. "It isn't safe for you to be here alone."

"I need to be near the store, and I have pets."

"You can bring them with you. I'll make sure you get to work at whatever time you want." He squeezed my hand. "I'm in danger, too. There's safety in numbers."

So they say. It might not be a bad idea to stay with him. Nobody got inside the building without

Mr. Appleton knowing. It would be safer than here. "What if Moses comes back?"

"I guarantee that fat cat will be waiting for you to come feed him."

He had an answer to all my questions. "Okay. Once McIlroy leaves, I'll grab a few things."

"Don't look as if you're going to the guillotine. You might actually enjoy yourself. The guest room is quite comfortable. I've replaced Dad's bed and don't have a problem sleeping in the master room now."

"That's a great idea," McIlroy said. "Things might've had a different ending if Miss Ashford had been home when the intruder broke in. I don't see anything out of place." He stabbed me with his gaze. "Have the two of you learned anything?"

"Several local businessmen wanted my father to sell the apartment complex and demolish this mall." Brad stood and pulled the Jumpdrive from his pocket. "Found this in the penthouse. He'd started moving his finances into different banks, which is why I thought he was going broke. I believe my father knew his life was in danger and did his best to make sure no one got it all." He dropped the drive into McIlroy's outstretched palm.

"Everything I learned at the women's-only night at the club definitely points to someone wanting to purchase the complex. Mr. Jenkins, Evans, Roberts...they're all suspects in my book. There's a lot of money to be had for someone." I lifted my chin, almost revealing my plan to find out whether any of them owned a bottle of Infamous. Instead, I kept my tongue.

I had no idea how to sneak into their homes. It would take some strategic planning, and the most strategic person I knew who also didn't mind stepping over the line was Shar.

After the detective left, I put the cats in carriers, packed up their food and litter box, a few toys, and then packed a small suitcase of my own. Since the lock on my front door was broken, I set my laptop on the clothes and zipped the suitcase.

"Ready?" Brad opened the door for me in the underground garage of the complex. "You look like you'll fall asleep on your feet."

"No more so than you." He was right. I'd never been so tired.

"I got snatches of naps between your visit and phone call." He smiled. "The guestroom stays made up, so all you have to do is slide between the sheets."

I glanced around the garage. Brad had punched in a code in order to raise the security bar, but anyone on foot could duck under. He also punched in a code for the elevator. "The only way in and out, unless you live here, is through the front door, right?"

"Sure. You can get into the garage, but you won't have access to the building without a code."

Which meant Mr. Appleton had to have seen whoever killed Mr. Armstrong..."Is there a night shift doorman?"

"Appleton. Foster has the earlier shift. After midnight, there's no doorman. You have to use the garage." His mouth opened, then closed, his eyes wide. "I know where you're going with this.

Appleton had to have seen the killer."

I nodded. "He opened the door for me when I arrived. Your father hadn't been dead more than a couple of hours."

"There'll be security footage, but I'm sure the police have already seen it." The elevator door opened on the penthouse floor.

"I didn't have to enter a code that day. The door was unlocked. Either your father knew his killer or the person had the code to the penthouse. We need to speak with Appleton." Unfortunately, it was now past midnight, and he'd gone home.

Brad led me to a bedroom almost as big as my apartment. Modern, clean lines, and a thick white comforter that promised warmth on a winter night. I placed my bag inside the closet, set up the cat's litter box in the guest bath, and released the two cats from the carriers Brad had set inside the door.

They both raced off to explore, no doubt following Moses's scent. I plopped on the mattress. Not only did I need to find the missing feline later, but I had work. It wasn't fair to lay everything on Heather all the time.

"Can I get you anything?" Brad asked.

"No, thank you. I'm going to bed. I need to be at work at eight."

He smiled and left, closing the door behind him.

I quickly undressed, donning my usual sleepwear of baggy shorts and loose-fitting tee shirt, then slid between luxurious sheets. I mentally added to my to-do list planning how to obtain access to our suspects' homes. I couldn't take Moses along, but I could search for the Infamous trail.

Despite the day's events whirling through my head, I drifted off to sleep, dreaming of the clubwomen's reaction when they discovered I'd slept in the penthouse.

Chapter 17

I choked back a sob and fell to my knees when Brad dropped me off at work the next morning. Curled up on the welcome mat was Moses. A fine white powder coated his paws. He protested when I scooped him into my arms and squeezed. "I was so worried about you. Where have you been?"

"Let's make sure the apartment is secure before opening shop." Brad, toolbelt in hand, hurried up the stairs. "I'll take the cat to my place before starting work myself."

"Are you sure?" I followed. "He can stay in the shop with me."

"He'll feel right at home at the penthouse." Brad smiled over his shoulder. "Plus, he'll be a lot safer."

True. I'd need Moses to confirm the killer's identity once I found him or her. I was leaning toward the murderer being a him.

Nothing looked disturbed in the apartment, so I left Brad to fix the broken lock while I headed to the shop. I set Moses on the counter and booted up my laptop seconds before Heather and Shar arrived.

My best friend's long face told me Bobby was still missing. Without a word, she set Robbie in the dog playpen, mumbling something about finding some puppies for him to play with.

Shar had no sooner turned the closed sign to read open when Mrs. Nelson entered with Greta. "I need an emergency grooming. A kid at the park threw gum in her hair."

"I'll fix her right up." Shar took the pet carrier from the distraught woman and hurried to the grooming station.

Mrs. Nelson sent a shocked look at Robbie. "You're taking children on consignment?"

I laughed. "That's Heather's son. She doesn't have a sitter."

The woman nodded and leaned closer. "I heard he's on the run."

"Where did you hear that?" Heather stopped at the edge of the counter, her arms full of wriggly poodle pups.

"It's all over town. There's even a notice in the drugstore window labeling him as a person of interest." She took one of the puppies. "Are these for sale? Greta would love a little sister."

"Yes, they are." Heather set the ones she still held in the pen with her son. "We now take in pets to sell. They've been checked over by a vet."

"I'll take this little sweetie." She headed for the products on display. "Not to worry you, Heather, but I heard the police aren't the only ones hunting for your husband. Seems he owes somebody a lot of money."

"Any idea who?" I asked.

"I'm not a private investigator, Trinity, just an observant listener." She plucked a pink rhinestone-studded collar off a hook.

A gossip described her better, but she might be able to tell us something to help solve this case so I let her talk. "Who did you hear it from?"

"I heard it from Mrs. Wimbledon at the hair salon yesterday. She heard if from Mrs. Greene who heard it from…" she tapped her finger against her lips. "A cousin, I think. You know how word spreads in this town."

A whole lot of gossip and nothing concrete.

"Here you go." Shar returned with Greta. "You can't even tell where I cut the gum out. I trimmed the rest of her to match. Her whiskers are a little shorter than normal, but they'll grow."

"Thank you. Meet your sister, Frenchie." She put the puppy in the carrier with Greta. "Be nice. You have to set an example."

I'd long become accustomed to my customers speaking to their pets as if they were children. I smiled, knowing I spoke to my cats the same way. "Good as new."

Mrs. Nelson paid for the grooming and the puppy, then bustled from the store, still cooing to her fur babies.

"Who is up for a haircut? I just had one." I glanced at my friends. "Seems there's a lot of talk about Bobby going on over there."

Shar patted her head. "I could do with a trim." She smiled. "Something short and sassy that will fit snug under a cap. We're going snooping tonight. Most of our suspects will be at the club. Make sure you have something black to wear, Trinity."

"That sounds dangerous," Heather said after Shar left.

"I need to find out who wears Infamous."

She gasped. "I gave Bobby a bottle of that last Christmas. A lot of men wear that scent."

"I know, and I seriously doubt your husband killed Mr. Armstrong." Bobby might be a lot of things, but a killer wasn't one of them. Unless he really had something to lose by Mr. Armstrong's business dealings. I narrowed my eyes. "Did he have a reason to kill?"

"No. He has his gambling problem to deal with, but I seriously doubt Brad's father was the type to lend money like a loan shark." She plopped into a chair. "My bet is he borrowed, or stole, from Roberts."

I leaned my elbows on the counter and sighed, feeling very much like a hamster on a wheel. Nothing was falling into place. Brad and the detective were right. Finding a bottle of cologne in someone's possession didn't mean they killed my friend. I needed a confession. My mind whirled with all the names of the men who might have wanted Mr. Armstrong dead. All businessmen. All patrons of the club. All with gorgeous, yet bitter, girlfriends. "I need to learn how to flirt," I mumbled.

"What?" Heather arched a brow.

"If I knew how to flirt, I could cozy up to the suspects at the club. Men talk to those types of women, don't they? Like boasting?"

Laughter burst from her. "You are the least likely person to act that way of anyone I know."

"Doesn't mean I can't." I threw a ball at her.

She caught it and tossed it into the pen with her son. "Just bat your eyes, lean close, and let them do all the talking. Act interested in what they have to say. That's it. Maybe toss your hair once in a while." She flicked her hair over her shoulder, adopted a soft smile on her lips, and fluttered heavily hooded eyes. "See?"

"Wow. I'd tell you anything if I was a man and you looked at me that way." I'd never get away with it.

"Practice on Brad." Giggling, she headed to open the door for the delivery man who juggled several boxes.

Brad would think I'd lost my mind. Sighing, I turned to check those needing reservations to board their pets. My face heated when Brad arrived to fetch Moses. I smiled, batted my eyes, and tossed my hair.

His brow furrowed. "You okay? Your face is red. Are you running a fever? Do you have something in your eye?" He reached for me.

"I'm fine," I muttered, stepping back. "See you later. I'm going out with Shar, so I'll be late."

"Why are you telling Brad you're going out?" Heather tilted her head. "What did I miss?"

I explained about my apartment being broken into and Detective McIlroy's suggestion I stay with Brad. "It's nothing."

"Oh, but it could be something." She winked

and started opening boxes. "You lucky girl."

A woman arrived with a litter of kittens to sell, then a while later, a man brought in some beagle puppies. Things were looking up for the business. Seems folks didn't mind sharing the income when I took over the task of finding buyers and making sure all the animals' first shots were taken care of.

I glanced at the far wall again. Definitely time to install display cases. I placed the call with promises they'd arrive tomorrow. An expensive purchase, but I'd have it paid off with the sale of the beagles. People from the south liked their floppy-eared hunting dogs.

At the end of the workday, I headed upstairs at the back of the shop and into my apartment to get ready for a night of breaking and entering with Shar. My, how my life had taken a turn. I think I preferred the mundane routine from before.

I dressed all in black and took a nap on the sofa while I waited for Shar. The last thing I needed was to be tired. What if we had to make a fast escape?

A knock on the door woke me. I put my eye to the peep hole and lost my breath for a second until I realized the masked person on the other side was Shar. Opening the door, I slipped out and locked it behind me. "Is this really a good idea?"

"It might shorten the suspect list." She led the way down the stairs to a dark sedan. "I didn't want anyone recognizing the Thunderbird, so I rented a car."

"What if they're home?" I slid into the front passenger seat.

"They won't be. They're gone every

Wednesday to the club. Why would they buck tradition now? Relax."

My mind spun with possibilities. We could be discovered, arrested, killed. I closed my eyes and concentrated on breathing.

"You doing Lamaze?"

My eyes popped open. "What?"

"You're breathing weird."

"I'm trying not to panic."

"Not working." She pulled onto a tree-lined street. "We walk from here."

"You act like you've done this before."

She shrugged. "I read a lot of books and watch a lot of TV. It's common sense, really."

We stopped next to a high hedge. "Are we going through that?"

"Can't go over it. Protect your face and eyes." She squeezed through, leaving me standing alone in the dark.

I quickly followed, pretty sure any exposed skin would sport scratches, and emerged onto a sloping, well-manicured lawn. At the top of the slight hill stood a plantation-style mansion.

A huge dog appeared silently at my side. I pointed my finger. "No."

"How did you know that would work?" Shar whispered.

"It's a mastiff. Smart, loyal, and they know we aren't bad guys." I had no idea if that was why we hadn't been torn to bits, but it worked for me. The dog padded after us to the house.

"Stay."

The dog sat.

"It isn't wearing a collar," Shar said. "Are you sure it lives here?"

"I'm not sure of anything." I watched wide-eyed as she pulled a set of lock-picking tools from the small backpack she wore. "What if there's an alarm?"

"We run." Her teeth flashed in the moonlight.

Not a very good plan. "Whose house?"

"Roberts." She inserted the tools in the lock. A few minutes later, a click sounded abnormally loud to my ears. When no alarm sounded, she pushed the door open.

"Could be a silent alarm."

"Hush, Debby Downer." She stepped inside, then motioned me forward. "Nice place for a single man. He must have hired an interior designer."

I agreed. The inside looked as if no one lived there. Everything in its place, colors of brown, red, and forest green. Definitely masculine. "Maybe the upstairs is where he spends most of his time."

"That's where I'm headed." Shar put a hand on the newel post to the sweeping staircase. "I don't think anyone is home."

It didn't appear that way. If Roberts had live-in staff, they'd be in bed and clueless.

I followed her upstairs, peering into rooms until we found the master bedroom. Next door to it was an office. Both rooms looked far more lived in than the downstairs. Leaving the bedroom to Shar, I entered the office and lowered myself into the leather office chair, studying the massive walnut desk in front of me.

Having no real clue as to what I was looking

for, I opened the bottom drawer. Multiple files in different colors filled the space. I flipped through, noting the names. When I spotted Bobby Langley, I realized these were employee files. My eyes almost popped out of my head when I spotted Alan Appleton. The doorman to Waterfall Luxury Apartments? Had he once worked for Roberts?

I spread the file on top of the desk and opened it. Appleton once worked as a driver for Roberts, delivering cars to the new owners or other auto lots owned by Roberts. Why quit such a job to be a doorman? It didn't make any sense to me.

"He definitely wears Infamous," Shar said. "The bottle is almost empty."

I'd never smelled it on him, but maybe he only wore the cologne to commit murder. "Appleton used to work for him." I tapped the file in front of me.

Shar frowned in the light of her flashlight. "That's weird, but come to think of it, he's only been a doorman for a year or so. Maybe he got tired of driving."

"Or maybe he wanted a new career as a spy for Roberts. Who knows more about what goes on in that building than the doorman?" I returned the file to the drawer and made sure everything was as it had been before I sat down. "Let's head to the next place."

I stood as the door downstairs opened.

Chapter 18

"But, Richard, he'll find out," A young woman whined.

I knew that voice. I'd spoken to her just the other day. Why was Mr. Jenkins' pretty young mistress visiting with Roberts at eleven p.m.?

Putting a finger to my lips, I motioned for Shar to follow me onto the second-floor landing where I could hear better. Summer moved past my line of sight, still beyond cute in sweatpants and a spaghetti-strap top. Gone were the fancy gown and carefully applied makeup. The woman below us looked every bit the country girl.

"I agreed to do this because you said you'd pay for college. Not only is Harold getting suspicious, but his wife is, too."

I raised my brows at Shar. This information might make our snooping worthwhile. If we didn't get caught.

"All you're there for is to keep your ears open and your mouth shut," Roberts said. "Your father owes me big time. Don't forget that."

"Haven't I satisfied his debt yet?"

"Not until you find that file."

What could Jenkins have that Roberts wanted? Was it possible that what he was looking for was also on the thumb drive Brad had?

"What makes you think he has it?"

"He spent a lot of time with Armstrong before someone whacked him. Armstrong found out about my...side business. I can't let that info get any further. Now shut up and do the job you're told to do. Don't come here anymore either. I don't need people finding out. That'll ruin your cover."

I shrank back as Roberts gave Summer a push toward the front door. "Take your dog with you."

"It isn't my dog." She glared up at him, her eyes widening as she caught sight of me and Shar perched behind the railing.

I put my finger to my lips and silently implored her not to say anything. With a hike of her chin, she sashayed out the door, laughing. "Good luck keeping all your secrets quiet, cuz."

Roberts called her something unflattering and slammed the door after her. Heavy footsteps sounded as he marched out of sight.

"How are we going to get out of here?" Shar whispered.

"I'm hoping a house this big has a back staircase. Come on."

All five bedrooms had their own ensuites but no back stairs. Footsteps coming up the stairs had me jumping into the nearest bathtub. Why didn't modern showers have curtains? Leaving Shar to plaster herself behind the door, I made myself as small as possible on the cool porcelain.

My cell phone vibrated from the front pocket of the hoodie I wore, sounding loud against the tub. I held my breath, releasing it as Roberts passed our hiding place, whistling.

Shar snapped her fingers and pointed.

I counted to ten. Not hearing Roberts returning, I climbed slowly from the tub as the door to the master bedroom closed.

Not one to miss an opportunity that might not come again, I raced on tiptoes down the stairs, Shar on my heels, and yanked open the front door.

An alarm blared.

An upstairs door opened.

"Who's down there?" Roberts demanded. "I'm calling the cops."

Shar gave me a two-hand shove in my back, sending me flying down the stairs. I fell to my knees, jumping back up like a spring toy, then raced for the hedge alongside the property, Shar and the dog right behind me.

"Did he recognize us?" I shoved through the hedge.

"All he would have seen was two people in black racing out the front door." She bent over, balancing her hands on her knees. "I'm out of shape. If we're going to keep doing these types of things, I need to start working out."

"I have no future plans on breaking and entering."

"That's good to know."

I shrieked and whirled, coming face-to-face

with McIlroy. "It isn't what it looks like."

"Really?" He crossed his arms. "What I see are two women dressed like robbers running from a house where the owner just called the police because he had an intruder."

"Well, that did happen, but we weren't there to steal anything. I promise."

"Then why were you there?"

Shar removed her cap and shook out her hair. It crossed my mind that she might have taken the same flirtation classes Heather had. She batted her eyes. "We're looking for a killer, Detective. We didn't find one, but we did find a blackmailer." Her eyes fluttered faster.

"Follow me. Quickly." He spun and hurried toward his squad car. "Get in before someone sees you." Once we were inside, the mastiff squeezing in with us, McIlroy drove up to the house.

"He isn't going to alert Roberts it was us, is he?" I widened my eyes.

"I hope not. I never took him for a traitor."

McIlroy shook his head. "I can hear you, and I owe you nothing; therefore, I can't be a traitor. I have to let Roberts know I've apprehended the intruders. He doesn't need to know it was the two of you. Keep your heads down."

He shoved open his door and approached the man on the porch. After a few minutes, he returned and drove away.

"Did he suspect anything?"

"No, said he knew someone was around because of the dog." He narrowed his eyes in the rearview mirror. "Is it yours?"

"No," I said. "Where would I keep such a large pet? You keep her."

"I don't have time for a dog."

"Well, I can't keep her," Shar said. "If Roberts saw me walking this beast, he'd know I was at his house."

"Can you drop me off at Waterfall Apartments?" I asked. "And maybe take this sweet dog somewhere until we figure out what to do with her?"

"Put her in the penthouse. I doubt Roberts pays that much attention to what you do." He pulled into the parking garage. "Ms. Carpenter, where's your car?"

"Back at Roberts' house." She grinned.

Sneaky woman. She'd devised a way to spend a little more time with the handsome detective. "See you in the morning, Shar." I winked and slid from the car, waving the dog to follow me. Poor Brad. Three cats and now a monster of a dog in his home. "Come on, Sheba. If you're going to stay a while, you might as well have a name." I pressed the button for the elevators.

The door opened and Mr. Appleton stepped out. "You're home late, Trinity."

"You're working late." I forced a smile and entered the elevator after he stepped out.

"Covering the first part of the second shift. I'm not one to let the opportunity to make a little more money pass me by." He eyed Sheba. "Big dog. Not sure she'll be allowed. Where did you find her?"

"She's a stray. I found her wandering around outside." There. Not a lie. "You know me and

149

animals. I couldn't leave her."

"You have a good heart." He smiled, gave me a salute, and headed across the garage.

The man didn't act like a killer. Hopefully, just because he worked for Roberts at one time didn't mean he was up to no good now. At least I hoped the man wasn't hiding behind a mask of kindness.

Brad opened the door to the penthouse, a look of relief on his face. "It's late. I was worried." His gaze moved to Sheba. "Who's this?"

"I'll explain everything inside." It was nice having someone waiting and worrying about me, other than four-legged friends, when I came home late. I could get used to this.

Sheba stopped as three hissing, growling cats arched their backs and hopped across the floor in front of her. With a sigh, she plopped down, resting her head on her paws. Trouble averted.

Pulling off the knit cap I wore, I toed off my gym shoes and plopped onto the sofa before telling Brad all that Shar and I had learned that evening, ending with McIlroy bringing me to the penthouse. "I'd say we had a rather productive evening." I propped my feet on the coffee table.

"The night could have ended very differently if Roberts would have had guard dogs or a gun." Brad sat next to me. "Next time, I should come with you."

I tilted my head. "Do you have a gun?"

"No, but I can buy one."

"And do what? Shoot our suspect?" I laughed, cupping his cheek. "Thank you, but we were fine."

"We keep saying we need to talk to Appleton,

but this confirms it. In fact, asking him some questions is our number-one priority." He leaned against the leather back of the sofa. "I've been so busy with the mall renovations I've let finding my father's killer fall mostly at your feet. I'm sorry. This is my responsibility."

I entwined my fingers with his. "I cared about your father, too. We're both doing what we can to determine who killed him and help McIlroy at the same time. How's the construction of the theater coming?"

"Fine." He gave a lopsided grin. "I hired Jenkins."

"There you go. One of our prime suspects right under your nose."

"That's a good way of looking at things." He squeezed my hand. "I'll be with him a lot every day when he comes to check on his workers. If he's up to something, I'm bound to find out."

"I'll let you concentrate on him. I can question Appleton and Summer Bassett. That young lady knows more than she's letting on, I guarantee it." The hardest part would be asking the right questions. Since she knew Shar and I had overheard her conversation with Roberts, there was no need for secrecy. Leaning over, I planted a kiss on Brad's cheek. "Goodnight. Thank you for letting us stay here."

"You're welcome." His eyes warmed. "By the way, what do I do with the small pony you brought with you? I'm sure she's hungry."

"A steak?" I grinned, pushing to my feet. "I'll bring some dog food home from work tomorrow."

I woke sometime after dark to three cats huddled on the bed with me, a large dog growling at my bedroom door, and the sound of something clicking at the front door. Without turning on a light, I tossed aside the sheet and met Brad in the hall. "What is it?"

"Someone's trying to get inside. Stay in your room."

I grabbed the nearest object at hand, a lamp, and held it like a weapon. "I'm not letting you face the intruder alone."

The noise at the front door grew louder. No one could reach the penthouse without a code. It had to be someone we knew.

When a large thump sounded, Brad yanked the door open.

Mr. Appleton lay in a heap on the padded carpet. His eyes fluttered open. He held up a sheet of paper, then his eyes closed again. It was at that moment that I saw the blood spreading across his chest. One breath, a second, then none.

"Hold on." Brad dropped to his knees and felt for a pulse. Not finding one, he started CPR.

"There's too much blood. He's gone."

Brad glanced at the bloodstained paper he held. "It's a set of numbers."

"What do the numbers mean?"

"I don't know, but I think he was trying to warn us about something."

My throat clogged. He really did seem to be a nice guy. "Does this mean he knows your father's killer?"

"I'd say that's a good assumption, and now he's

become the next victim."

"He didn't say anything?" McIlroy stared at the numbers in his hand a few minutes later.

"Just handed us that," Brad said, wiping his bloody hands on a wet rag I'd grabbed from the kitchen. "Could be a combination, a bank account number...one number short from a phone number."

McIlroy scratched his head. "We're not getting anywhere on this case."

I agreed. The one man who might have had some answers now lay in a black bag outside the door. Poor Mr. Appleton. My next move would be talking to Summer Bassett.

Chapter 19

"What makes you think she'll talk?" Shar handed Moses to me. "I don't know why you brought the cats to work with you. This one in particular gets into everything."

"I miss them." I snuggled his fuzzy orange fur, then set him on the counter. "As for Summer, she knows we overheard her conversation with Roberts. She's probably wondering what's taking us so long to ask her questions."

"Maybe." She pursed her lips. "Too bad about the doorman. A fountain of information is what got him killed. What were the numbers? Maybe we can figure out what they mean."

Since I'd memorized them, I scratched them on a pad of paper I kept by my laptop. 243627.

"I'd bet Moses's tail that's a combination to a lock." Shar nodded like a bobblehead doll. "Where do people use combinations?"

"The gym?"

"Bingo. Looks like we're going to work out

after work. Evans Fitness finished moving in next door, right? Perfect time to act curious about what services they offer."

"I don't like going to the gym."

"You won't be skinny all your life if you don't start exercising." Shar turned to open the door for Heather. "You really need to get a babysitter."

"I know." Heather sighed. "The people putting up the cages for the animals for sale are here. I'll have to keep Robbie in the grooming room so he's out of the way."

"Here." Brad squeezed in before Shar could close the door. "He can come with me to the theater. I'll buy him an ice cream later."

A look of relief flickered across her face. "Are you sure?"

"Yep. We'll be just fine together." He tossed me a wink. "See you later?"

My face warmed. "I'll be a little late. Shar wants me to check out the gym next door with her after work."

"It's a nice place. I popped in yesterday. I can put you on my membership if you want. Say bye, Robbie."

Heather's son waved and grinned, clearly excited to be leaving with Brad. Too bad it wasn't his father caring for him for the day.

"Hold onto that one," Shar said. "He's a good man."

Unfortunately, he wasn't mine to hold onto. I moved some standing display shelves out of the arriving workers' way, then perched on a stool behind the counter to supervise. Twelve glass cases with just enough room to move behind in order to feed and remove the animals would take up valuable space in my shop. I'd have to be creative in displaying my other products.

The yipping of the puppies in the pen and the hammering of the workers combined to give me a killer of a headache within a half an hour. "I'm going to the bookstore to buy coffee. Either of you want one?" I pushed off the stool.

Shar and Heather both declined. Outside, the warm morning sun caressed my face, easing some of the stress of construction. Not all of the stress, though, as noise blasted from the theater where construction happened on a much larger scale.

I waved to Brad who stood next to the stroller speaking with Harold Jenkins. Both men waved back before returning to their conversation. I passed the sparkling clean windows of the new gym, noticing other improvements in the mall as I strolled down the sidewalk. Burned-out bulbs in signs had been replaced, outside walls sported new coats of paint, and someone had even painted an open book on the big bookstore window.

Brad was a man of his word, improving the mall without raising rent. That would come, though, as the stores made bigger profits. I couldn't fault him when it did. He was a businessman above all else. Funny how the idea of a larger rent didn't fill me with dread as it once had. My income had started to grow. Since business was good, I wasn't even sure I still wanted to be a veterinarian. Why spend all that money when things were fine as they were? Chuckling at how my mind had changed, I entered the bookstore.

Mrs. Ansley grinned from behind the coffee bar. "Good morning. You look happy."

"Just thinking about all the changes happening."

"Good ones, I think. The usual? Mr. Armstrong bought me new coffee equipment in exchange for free coffee for the rest of his life." She grinned. "Not so free when he bought the things needed to make the coffee, but I'm not fool enough to say no. He also said coffee was free for you, too." She wiggled her eyebrows. "Tongues are starting to wag about the two of you."

"Oh?" Other than the tongues at Women's Night at the club? "Where are people talking?"

"Here, the hair salon, the grocery store—everywhere jealous women gather." She laughed. "I'm teasing. The people who've talked about you aren't envious, merely curious." She set my frozen mocha coffee on the counter. "So? What is going on between the two of you? Don't say nothing. You're living in the penthouse with him."

"Only until my apartment is considered safe to return to after someone broke in."

She raised an eyebrow. "If I were you, I'd push that day back as far as possible."

Now that my face had to be the color of a cherry tomato, I nabbed my drink and rushed back to the noise of my store. Shoving open the door, I skidded to a halt at the sight of Summer Bassett smiling in my direction. She held one of the poodle puppies in her arms.

"Mrs. Nelson showed me her darling new baby, and I simply had to have one. My apartment gets lonely sometimes."

I glanced over her shoulder to where Shar watched through the window, the handheld faucet to wash dogs spraying the glass. I shook my head and turned back to Summer. "Poodles are awesome. Sweet and they don't shed. You'll love this little guy."

"What should I buy for him?" She studied a dog bed. "Food, toys, that sort of thing. When I was little, my father took care of the animals."

"I'll make a pile of the things you'll need. How about a book on potty training?"

"Perfect." She followed me around the store as I tossed things in a basket. Then, "I need your help," she whispered.

"What?" I narrowed my eyes. "With the dog? You can always bring him here during the day if you're worried about leaving him while you go to work."

"Not that." She shook her head. "With Roberts." The s on the end of his name hissed through her teeth. "You heard my conversation with him. I've looked everywhere for the evidence he wants and always come up empty."

"You mean about his stealing and reselling cars?"

"You know about that?"

"Everybody knows about that." Well, maybe not everyone since the man wasn't in jail. I added a ball to the basket and carried it to the counter. "Just tell your cousin you've come up empty-handed. If Mr. Jenkins hasn't told you anything derogatory about Roberts, then maybe he doesn't have the proof your cousin thinks he does."

"Did Mr. Armstrong ever mention anything before he died?"

"No, we talked mostly about his cat." I rang up her purchases, including the puppy. "Are you worried for your safety, Summer? Because if you are, you need to let the police know. Maybe go to the pound and adopt a big dog. This little guy won't be much of a deterrent."

"My cousin would never harm me." She gave a shaky smile. "I'll tell him that no one seems to know about his side business. Thanks."

The door hadn't closed behind the young woman when Shar joined me. "I'll dry the glass later. What did she want?"

"To buy a puppy." I glanced at the workers. One in particular seemed interested in our conversation. I lowered my voice. "Come to the office. I'll fill you in. Heather, can you manage here?"

She nodded, then continued to fill a jar of dog treats. "Not a lot to do today."

In the office, we sat, and I let Shar know what Summer had told me. "It really isn't much."

"No, it isn't. What a disappointment. I'd hoped she'd have something concrete to give us." She drummed her fingers on the arm of the chair. "I guess we're back to going to the gym after work."

"Yippee." I didn't even own workout clothes. "I'll have to go to the thrift shop and find some yoga pants."

"Don't look like your dog died. You can walk on the treadmill. It really isn't that bad." Shar reached over and patted my hand. "Go get yourself something cute. Working out is always easier if you look good doing it."

So, I found myself strolling down the sidewalk again. I glanced at the theater not seeing Brad, Robbie, or Mr. Jenkins. Had the older man seen his mistress enter Tail-Waggin'? Would he even care?

At the thrift store, Mrs. Murdock led me to a rack full of exercise clothes. "I always get a lot of donations this time of year. People make resolutions in January and donate the things they just bought a few months later."

I chose a pair of black leggings that went to my knees. A pink stripe down the side of each leg gave it a bit of color. A matching top went into my basket, then I added another set in black and orange. Two outfits ought to do me since I didn't plan on making the gym a regular habit.

Fifteen dollars poorer, I carried my purchases back to the store where Brad had returned Robbie. "How'd the babysitting go?"

"He's a good little guy, but now that your pet cases are installed, I need to do some things inside the theater. Too much construction for a little boy to be around." He ruffled Robbie's hair. "It was fun watching him. See you at the gym." He strode out the door.

I widened my eyes. Shar must have invited him to join us. Now I'd have to huff, puff, and sweat around Brad. Things were looking worse and worse. With a sigh, I set my bag under the counter and moved kittens and puppies for sale into their cases. Three kittens and four beagles, plus the two remaining poodles, left me with a lot of empty cases. Time to put a notice in the local paper and online.

At four o'clock, I left Heather to lock up the store and headed upstairs to wash the workout clothes and then change. I might not be sleeping in my apartment, but most of my things were there, which meant I regularly climbed the stairs for something. The outside door hadn't been opened since Brad repaired the lock.

At five-thirty, I joined Shar and Brad on the sidewalk. "Let's get this over with."

Brad flipped my ponytail. "You look cute."

I wouldn't look cute within half an hour. When I exercised, I turned bright red, and not just my face. My arms and neck could be seen from space once I got heated. "Let's get this over with and find out whether we're right about the combination."

Chapter 20

The inside of Evans Fitness smelled of sweat, deodorant, with an underlying whiff of new rubber. My palms immediately started to sweat, and I clutched the tattered backpack containing clean clothes to change into after I showered.

"Relax, Darlin'. It won't kill you." Brad's breath tickled my neck as he leaned close to whisper. Then, straightening, he faced the girl behind the counter. "Susie, I'd like to add these two ladies to my membership."

Her grin widened. "Sure thing. All they need to do is fill out these forms and I'll get their cards made." She peeled off two sheets from a pad of enrollment forms, plucked two pens from a basket, and slid the lot across the counter. "Would you like the platinum level so they can enjoy the water massage and tanning beds?"

"Yes, give them the works." He smiled at me, then headed for the men's dressing room.

How could he look so happy to be here? "Don't

forget about the combination!" I called out.

He raised a hand, then disappeared through an opening in the wall under a huge sign reading Men.

Now the proud owner of a tiny card that hooked on a keyring, I followed Shar to the women's changing room and stored my backpack in a locker. "What do we do? Go around and try the combination on every single lock?" There had to be a hundred, and that was in the common area, not counting the elite lockers.

"Grab your pack. We're in the wrong place." Shar reached out and grasped the shiny handle on a glass door. "Lockers are provided on platinum. My guess is the combination will fit one of the elite lockers in either the women's or men's. Try and act like you belong. You're with Brad, after all."

Excuse me if my name wasn't on the Social Register. "We aren't together."

"You're the only one in town who believes that." She placed her glittery yellow gym bag into a locker.

Shrugging off my poor backpack, I chose a different locker. "How will I know the combination?"

Shar thought for a moment, then looked at her membership card. "There's instruction on the back on how to set it. Now that these lockers are ours as long as we belong to this gym, no one else can change the lock. Clever."

Quickly setting my code to something I could remember, I closed the door and turned to study the walls of other lockers. "I'll start at one end, and you take the other. Act innocent if someone enters."

"Can't we work out first?" Shar scowled.

"There's no one else in here right now. You can go if you want and I'll search by myself." That would get me out of sweating.

"No, it'll be faster if I help." She started punching buttons in locker after locker.

If someone entered, she plopped on the padded bench and started whistling. She wasn't fooling anyone.

"Excuse me?" Susie joined us. "The two of you have been in here a long time and several people have mentioned they thought you were trying to steal from the other lockers."

Shar hitched up her chin. "The opposite, in fact. We're testing the security of these locks. Mr. Evans has done a fine job." She grabbed a towel from a basket and sashayed out the door.

Doing my best to keep my smile from trembling, and failing, I dashed out after Shar. When I saw her shaking some heavy-looking rope things, I switched directions and chose a treadmill. Oh, yay. Televisions turned to many different channels would keep me entertained. I stuck ear pods in my ears, turned on the machine to a nice slow pace, and watched a show on decorating.

The gym started to fill up. Jenkins entered, then a few minutes later, Summer followed. Amber Stirling waltzed in as if being Evans' girlfriend made her queen of the gym. She glanced my way after checking in and speaking with Susie. Uh-oh.

Pasting a smile on her face, Amber headed my way, stepping onto the treadmill next to me. "Good evening." She turned hers to a running speed, her ponytail bouncing on her shoulders. "Enjoying yourself?"

"Sure." I narrowed my eyes. How could she run and talk?

"Susie said you were having some trouble with the lockers." Her gaze sharpened. "Get it straightened out?"

"Yep."

Summer chose the treadmill on the other side of me, making me feel very much like a sandwich on the verge of being cut into tiny pieces. "Hey, Trin. Amber. It's nice having a gym so close, isn't it? Maybe now, Harold will get into shape."

"Where is he?" I glanced around.

"Holed up with Evans, most likely." She shrugged. "There might be some last-minute work Joe wants to hire him for. The two have been meeting a lot lately."

"We aren't to talk about what our men do, Summer." Amber slowed her machine, an icy look creeping across her features. "You're breaking the rules by talking to Trinity."

"But she's with Brad. She's one of us." Summer paled.

"Not really." I flashed a smile and cut off my machine. The area roped off for a thirty-minute workout looked promising and, hopefully, more solitary. "Have a great workout." I hopped from the machine and headed across the gym, waving at Brad who lifted weights.

The thirty-minute workout was sixty seconds of different weight machines and steps for cardio. I could do this for a half an hour, right? Shar could be right. Though I might be small now, I was approaching thirty and could start packing on the pounds any day. I squared my shoulders and got to work.

Fifteen minutes into it, I felt as if I'd been through the wringer, my ponytail sticking to my neck. By the time the half hour was over, I swore never to do anything more than the treadmill again and headed for the showers. The water-massage bed was looking mighty good now.

Passing Shar, who had moved onto some torture-type machine that worked her abs, I pointed to the women's showers. She nodded and kept pumping. I retrieved my pack from the locker and headed to the sauna. After stripping down, I wrapped myself in an extra-large towel and stepped into the wood-paneled room, smelling heavily of eucalyptus. Summer slumped on one corner of the bench.

"You okay?" I asked, sitting across from her.

"I really did think you were one of us."

"Brad and I are just friends. No worries. You haven't told me anything incriminating. Did you talk to your cousin?"

She nodded. "He's finally convinced Jenkins doesn't know anything. I should leave this life behind and go home to Oklahoma. I'd miss the luxury, but at least I'd like myself again." Summer stiffened, clamping her lips together as Amber entered the sauna.

The woman shot Summer a sharp look, which she quickly replaced with a friendly expression aimed at me. "I apologize if I made you uncomfortable earlier."

"You didn't." I tightened my towel around me, clearly not feeling comfortable now. The woman had a predatory gleam in her eyes as if she enjoyed being passive-aggressive. I refused to be intimidated and forced myself to stay put as Amber scolded Summer on the proper behavior for the girlfriend of a man as prominent as Jenkins.

I rolled my eyes and pretended to study my toes.

"I'm glad to see you at the gym. It's important always to look your best, and that means keeping fit." Amber peered closer at the other woman. "I can see your roots. Regardless," she shrugged, "pillow talk is kept secret. Always. Things happen to girls who don't remember that." Amber sprang to her feet and left.

"That sounded like a threat, didn't it?" Summer asked. "Should I be worried?"

"Maybe it was just a warning. Not really something to worry about." Although it sounded very much like a threat. "Think I'll hit the shower. I've had enough of this eucalyptus heat."

A cool shower felt wonderful after the sauna, and since it wasn't my water, I took my time, slowly heating the water to almost hot and letting it ease the tightness in my shoulders. I liked Summer. She might be almost ten years younger, but she still held onto a bit of naivety that I hoped wouldn't get her into trouble, considering the circles she traveled in.

I lathered my hair with the citrus-scented shampoo provided. Joe Evans had thought of everything, or maybe it was Amber. Either way, luxury products in the women's showers were a definite plus in my book.

As I turned off the water, the lights went out, pitching me into complete darkness. The only sound was the spray of a shower further down the line of stalls. "Hello? A little help, please?" I couldn't see my hand in front of my face.

I fumbled for my backpack, being careful not to slip on the wet tile in search of my cell phone. There. I illuminated the screen and peered through the part in the curtain. The water still ran in the other stall.

I called Shar. "Can you inform the front desk that the lights have gone out in the women's showers? It's dangerously dark, and I'm afraid to leave the stall."

"I'll do that right now. Stay put. Of course, if you were to fall, you could sue and pay off all your debts." She laughed and hung up.

I shook my head and wrapped myself in a towel, sitting on the small stool in the stall's corner. Strange how noise amplified in the dark. From the other stall came a thud. Maybe they'd dropped something. "Are you okay?" I called out.

No one answered, but they sure liked long showers. I peeked through the curtain and caught sight of a pen light disappearing around the corner. "Hey, I could use some help, please." Not receiving an answer, I resumed my seat.

Finally, the lights flickered back on. Thank you, God. I dried off, dressed, and grabbed my things. Still wearing cheap flip-flops instead of going barefoot, I stepped out and glanced at the drain in the center of the room.

A slim river of red ran from the other stall, joining with the water swirling down the drain. I recognized blood when I saw it. Setting my things on the counter, I shoved aside the curtain of the other stall, thinking the occupant might have slipped and fallen in the dark.

I was partially right. Summer slumped in the corner, a knife protruding from her back.

"Help!" I cut off the water and dropped to my knees, feeling for a pulse. Still alive. "Help me!"

"What is it?" Shar, wrapped in a towel, rushed to my side. "Oh."

"Call the police and an ambulance." I took the towel Summer had hung on a hook and folded it into a makeshift pillow, then lowered her to her side, being careful not to jostle the knife.

Whoever had held that tiny light had tried to kill Summer Bassett. My suspicion ran to one woman, Amber in particular, but with the lights off a man could have come in and done the deed.

My blood chilled. I could just as easily have been the one lying there with a knife in my back.

Chapter 21

Joe Evans, Amber, Brad, and Shar darted into the women's room. Brad wrapped me in his arms and cradled my head against his chest. The tremors that had come with the realization I could have been attacked started to subside.

By the time McIlroy and the paramedics arrived, I felt more like myself and ready to answer questions. The paramedics went straight to Summer while the detective made a beeline for me.

"Let's talk somewhere more private," he said, leading me to the glassed-in room where the elite lockers were. "Out!" He pointed toward the door when Shar tried to squeeze through.

"Meanness makes you less attractive, Detective." Nose in the air, she left, closing the glass door behind her, then stood, arms crossed, glaring through the glass.

"Can Brad stay, please?" I wasn't ready to release the feeling of safety I had when he was by my side.

"I do have something of interest to tell you," Brad said.

"Fine." McIlroy pulled out his pad and pencil. "I regret having asked you to get involved in the case, Miss Ashford. Things are escalating too quickly for your safety."

I agreed in theory but really wanted to see things through to completion. Whoever killed Mr. Armstrong was still out there. I seriously doubted it was the same person who tried to kill Summer, but maybe the same killer did both. Deaths were definitely piling up in the once safe town of Waterfall.

"Is this what big business does?" I tilted my head. "Bring death, destruction, and poor morals to a place?"

Both men stared at me as if I'd suddenly turned purple. "Think about it. It wasn't until all the improvements started, the apartment complex was built, and that country club opened up in Silver Brook that this town changed."

"Probably had something to do with it. Now, tell me what happened." The detective's pencil hovered over the pad.

"First, you should know that Amber scolded Summer about leaking things considered pillow talk to me. Summer didn't tell me anything that would warrant that type of reaction from Amber, but she did tell me the other night that her cousin, Richard Roberts, wanted her to find out if Jenkins knew anything about his side business." I widened my eyes. "You do know about the stealing and reselling of cars, right?"

He nodded. "Don't have enough proof right now to convict, though. Continue."

"Summer came in to shower after I was already in my stall. I thought the water ran a long time but shrugged it off. Then the lights went out, I heard a thud, called for help, saw a light, then waited. After the lights came on, I got dressed and stepped out of the stall. That's when I saw the blood coming from Summer's shower. I checked on her, saw the knife, and that's it."

"You saw a light?"

"Like from a tiny flashlight. Whoever stabbed her made sure they were the only one who could see through the dark."

"You couldn't tell anything about the person with the light?"

"Nope. Sorry." I leaned against Brad. "It's really dark in there when the lights go out."

"What did you find out, Mr. Armstrong?"

"The location of the lock that matches the numbers Appleton gave us. It's a locker in the men's elite room. I opened the locker, but it was empty. The front desk said it belonged to Bobby Langley, but he left days ago."

Why would Appleton have the combination to Bobby's locker? "My friend's husband might be a lot of things, but he isn't a murderer." I scowled. Heather was going to have a meltdown.

"Do we have a clue where he is?" Brad asked.

"The man seems to have disappeared into thin air." McIlroy closed his pad and slipped it into his pocket. "Be careful, you two. Maybe step back and stop asking questions. That was a lapse in judgment on my part. Call me if you remember anything else."

"But we've found out more than the police." I shook my head. "I won't stop until Mr. Armstrong's murderer is brought to justice."

"I'll keep an eye on her." Brad's arm tightened around me. "I'm a good shot and don't have a problem carrying a gun."

"I've created monsters." Shaking his head, McIlroy left only to be replaced by Shar.

"I'm having second thoughts about pursuing that man. If he won't let me be a part of things, I'm not sure what kind of future we have. Tell me what's going on?"

"Not here." I pushed to my feet. "How about we head to my apartment and I make coffee? I need to get some clothes to take to the penthouse anyway, and I want to talk to Heather. Maybe she'll meet us there." I sent her a quick text telling her it was urgent.

By the time we stepped outside, Heather replied she could be there in five minutes because she was getting her hair done. Wonderful. Somewhere in the recesses of her mind, she had to have an idea where her husband was hiding.

"I'll fix the coffee," Brad said inside my apartment. "You've had a traumatic experience, and Shar is champing at the bit to be filled in."

While he headed to my tiny galley kitchen, I told Shar everything that had happened after my workout. Her eyes widened to the point I thought they might fall out. "All this while I was working out? Girl, you have all the excitement."

"You can have it. I've never been more scared in my life." I got up to let Heather in. "Who's watching the baby?"

"The neighbors, so I have to make this quick. What's up?"

I quickly filled her in on the night's events, including the gym locker that had been in Bobby's name. "Did you know he had a membership?"

"Yes, but he canceled it once I found out about our money problems." She plopped into a chair. "He wouldn't have killed anyone, but he might know something that could get him killed. Especially after working for Roberts."

"Where would he hide?"

She sucked her bottom lip between her teeth. "I'm not sure, but he wouldn't leave town. He'd want to stay close in case I needed him. Even after our fight, Bobby would want to keep me safe."

Too bad he didn't consider that before breaking the law. Still, Heather was my best friend. I wouldn't hurt her by saying what I really thought of her husband. "Think. You must know something."

Brad handed Shar and me each a cup of coffee. "Heather?"

"No thanks. I won't be able to sleep if I have some." She nibbled her lips, then gasped. "His grandmother's house. No one has lived there for years. It's about ten miles out of town and surrounded by trees. A person could hide there easily enough."

"Can you draw us a map?" Excitement coursed through me. Hopefully, she was right, and Bobby could fill in some blanks. I stood to retrieve the notebook I kept in a kitchen drawer and handed it to her.

"The hardest part will be seeing it at night through all the trees and thick underbrush. It's been neglected, sad to say." She drew a crude map. "If you find my husband, please tell him to turn himself in, so I don't have to worry anymore."

"Most definitely." I glanced at Brad, who nodded.

"I'll drive."

Shar clapped. "At least I'm not missing out on all the fun."

Heather stared at her for a minute, then shrugged. "You're a little crazy, aren't you?"

"Yep. I'm the one a normal family would have kept locked in the attic." She glanced at Brad. "What are we waiting for?"

"For y'all to climb in the car, I guess." Brad grinned and set his half-empty cup in the sink. "Let's go find our runaway."

"Keep me posted," Heather said. "I'll keep my phone next to the bed."

Five minutes later, we were in Brad's Mercedes, Shar oohing and aahing over the leather seats. "Gorgeous car, but I still prefer my Thunderbird."

Brad glanced in the rearview mirror. "I'd buy that car if you ever want to sell."

"Not while I'm still breathing."

He laughed and pulled out of the parking lot. "Okay, map reader, where to?"

"Take I-40 east," I said, "then take the London exit." After that, Heather had drawn pictures of landmarks. I hoped we'd be able to see them in the growing darkness.

"Right there. Is that a yellow mailbox?" I peered out the window a while later.

"I think so," Shar said.

Brad turned the wheel, taking us down a side road. "Are all the landmarks going to be like this?"

"Yep. You're going to turn left at a tree that has a trunk in the shape of a Y." I grinned. "Then turn left again at a barn full of woodpecker holes. There's a dirt road. The cabin is at the end of it."

"I don't like taking my car down dirt roads." Brad cut a quick glance my way.

"I'm not the one who put it there. I'm simply reading the map." If I owned the Mercedes, I might cringe too with rocks pinging the undercarriage and trees reaching out with skeletal fingers to scratch the paint.

The cabin looked deserted. Rundown was nowhere close to being an apt description. If Bobby was here, he'd been roughing it for days.

Brad left the car running and the headlights aimed on the house to provide us with light. "Bobby Langley? It's Brad Armstrong and Trinity Ashford."

"You shouldn't be here!"

"We need to talk to you, Bobby." I stepped onto the porch. "Heather is worried sick, and Mr. Appleton is dead. He gave us the combination to your locker, but it's empty."

"Of course, it's empty." He joined me on the porch. "I couldn't go on the run and leave evidence behind. That would be stupid."

"What kind of evidence? You need to turn

yourself in and take whatever you have to the police." I put my hand on his shoulder. "Think of your family. Things could get dangerous for them."

"That's why I left." Bobby shrugged me off. "I have proof that Jenkins cuts corners on his construction jobs. He made a fortune building that fancy apartment complex. Mr. Armstrong discovered that some of the corners he cut could be safety issues. He confronted Jenkins with the blueprints. That's the last time anyone saw your father alive."

"How did my father get ahold of those blueprints?" Brad asked.

"He gathered them up from all over town as part of his reconstruction. Some of those old buildings have tunnels and secret walls. If you study a blueprint enough, you can discover the discrepancy." Bobby sagged against the dilapidated wall. "Give me a moment, and I'll get the stuff and have you drop me off at the police station. I'm tired of running."

"Wait a minute," Shar said. "Isn't it strange that a car mechanic knows all this? I mean, call me suspicious, but why you, Bobby?"

Good question. How did a gambling mechanic who stole cars on the side team up with Mr. Armstrong?

His wide eyes darted from me, to Shar, to Brad. "It's no secret that I'm in a financial bind. Mr. Armstrong caught me trying to steal his car. At first, he thought Roberts might be in partnership with Jenkins, but I didn't find any evidence of that. In exchange for not turning me into the police, he asked me to keep tabs on Roberts, then I started doing odd jobs for Jenkins. I found the blueprints behind a wall I tore down in his shed. Jenkins had hired me to renovate it."

"That doesn't make sense. Why hide something that important, then hire someone to tear down the wall hiding it?" I crossed my arms.

"I wasn't supposed to tear down walls, just patch holes and paint." He sighed. "I noticed the loose drywall and pulled it back enough to see something had been shoved in there." Bobby ran his hands through his hair. "I'm done. Take me in. At least prison has flushing toilets and hot showers."

It looked every bit like Jenkins killed Mr. Armstrong. Did that mean it was Amber who'd stabbed Summer in the shower? All because Bobby had stumbled across blueprints that showed Jenkins hadn't done his job properly?

I shook my head. At least things were wrapping up. McIlroy could take it from here.

Chapter 22

"**I don't have** any proof you got these from Jenkins' property." McIlroy scowled. "While I'm glad you came to your senses and turned yourself in, this isn't enough evidence to suggest he killed Armstrong."

"What do you mean? This is proof!" I stomped my foot for emphasis. "What more do you need?"

"This shows Jenkins is a corrupt businessman, not that he's a murderer."

"What do you want, a picture of him committing the crime? A taped confession?"

McIlroy's face darkened. "We'll be questioning Mr. Jenkins in hopes he says something incriminating. It's late, Miss Ashford. Go home."

"We aren't going home," Brad said, the instant we got in the car. "If the detective wants proof, we'll find proof."

"How?"

Shar leaned over the seat. "You going to confront Jenkins?"

"He's out of town." Brad started the car. "We're going to do some snooping around his house."

"Now, you're talking." Shar sat back in the seat and clicked her seatbelt into place. "Of course, I'm not really prepared. This pink shirt isn't exactly subtle."

"It won't matter. If someone starts asking questions, I'm there in regard to the theater."

"You'll have to make sure he isn't cutting corners there, too." I put my hand on his arm.

"Yep. Looks like I'll be firing Jenkins and bringing in a new construction crew. Hopefully, one I can trust." My law-abiding friend stomped the gas pedal and pealed rubber out of the police station parking lot.

"I'm sorry, Brad." My heart ached for him. "We thought this was over and you'd get justice for your dad."

"Oh, it will be, even if I have to serve justice myself."

"I didn't figure you for a vigilante," Shar said.

"I'm not. I'll find that evidence McIlroy wants."

I had the feeling "or die trying" was tacked onto the end of his comment. "We're here to help. I won't stop either."

"Neither will I," Shar said. "We're a team."

"You two are the best friends a man could ask for."

Mere friends? I knew all those opinions about us being an item were wrong. The confirmation nicked at my heart a bit. I wouldn't mind being Brad's girl.

Jenkins lived in a large two-story house on the outskirts of town surrounded by acres of cleared pastureland holding a few head of long-horned cattle. His nearest neighbor was separated by barbed wire fence and a line of pine trees.

"Perfect." Brad shoved his door open. "Chances are no one will see us. His wife went out of town with him. There shouldn't be anyone here."

With a back as straight as one of the pines on the property, Brad led us around the house to the back door. "Don't disappoint me, Shar. Can you pick this lock?"

She laughed. "You betcha, handsome boy." Shar dug in her person for the tools. "I wasn't always the sweet, upstanding citizen you see before you."

I didn't doubt that for a second. "What about an alarm?"

"We'll worry about that if it happens," Brad said. "Most folks out here don't believe they need one. Everybody has a gun instead."

True. They usually had a dog or two, but I didn't see one and mentioned the fact.

"Jenkins' wife hates animals." Brad opened the door once we heard the loud click of the lock opening. "I'm going to search the office."

"Shouldn't someone dig through the shed where Bobby found the blueprints?" I asked. "There aren't a lot of places Jenkins would hide incriminating evidence. We should also be checking the construction office."

"We'll go there next. Why don't you and Shar check out the shed?"

I nodded, doubting we'd find anything more after Bobby's work, but I didn't want to leave any stone unturned. Glad I wouldn't be searching the shed at the back of the property by myself, I led Shar across the mowed grass and waited while she worked her magic on the shed lock.

Inside, I flicked on the light and stared at the cleanest shed I'd ever seen. Lawn tools hung on a freshly painted wall the color of spring grass. A counter stretched along one wall and held pots for planting. Under the counter were bags of potting soil. "This isn't a man's shed. It has to be his wife's gardening hub."

"That's why he thought the blueprints would be safe here," Shar said. "No one would suspect Jenkins of hiding something in what is clearly his wife's space."

Which made me think again of the construction office. "Let's check on Brad. We won't find anything here that points to Jenkins killing Mr. Armstrong. After Bobby found the evidence of his shoddy work, he'd have chosen a new hiding place."

The interior of the Jenkins home looked professionally decorated in country chic. Someday, I wanted a home like this. At the rate I collected pets, my apartment was straining at the seams. Mr. Jenkins' office, on the other hand, was strictly male right down to the twelve-point buck head mounted on the wall.

"Find anything?" I asked.

Brad shook his head and closed a desk drawer. "I think you're right. Anything we might need will be at the construction site."

"Will it be guarded?"

"If it is," Shar said, "I'll distract the guard. I have that way about me."

"How?" I arched a brow.

"I'm a poor defenseless woman who has car trouble. Take me to my Thunderbird, and I'll follow you. No man can resist that car, especially if I'm in the driver's seat."

A person had to admire her hubris. "It's as good a plan as any." I admired her creativity.

Half an hour later, Shar drove onto the construction office lot while Brad parked on the main road. "We'll be walking in, so we can sneak around while the guard is occupied."

From the protection of a couple of juniper bushes, we watched as the guard popped the hood on Shar's car. I had no idea what'd she done to make the car appear to be having trouble, but as long as it gave us time to search the office, I didn't care.

"Come on." Brad took my hand.

Staying bent over, we jogged to the construction trailer. "What's he building here?" I asked.

"I don't know. He's always got a few projects going, although the theater is his largest at this time." He reached up and wiggled the doorknob. "Darn it. We need Shar to pick the lock."

"No, she handed me her tools when we dropped her off at her car." I handed him the little black box. "You can figure it out. I'll stand watch." While he fiddled with the lock, I plastered my back to the aluminum siding of the trailer and peered around the corner.

Shar laughed at something the guard said. He

did seem more interested in her than checking the engine. My middle-aged friend still had what it took to keep a man's attention.

"We're in." Brad tapped my shoulder. "We need to move fast."

"Got it." I stepped into a sterile office and shined a flashlight on metal furniture and filing cabinets. Not believing Jenkins would have anything incriminating in something as obvious as a filing cabinet, I rifled through a few boxes stacked in the corner with the word Archive written across them.

Where would his archives be? A storage unit? Eventually, we had to run out of places to search, right? Come on, Jenkins. Where's the evidence?

"This is a waste of time," Brad said. "It's not like the man would have written down somewhere that he had committed murder. In my opinion, knowing my father was privy to what Jenkins was up to is enough for me."

"We need to get a confession out of him. Summer might have helped us, but she's out of commission for a while."

"Shar?"

"Too old for the man's taste."

"You?"

I shuddered. "I'm no good at flirting." And I definitely wouldn't let things progress further than simple flirtation. "Maybe you could trip him up when he's working on the theater?"

"That does seem our best bet at this time."

I gripped his arm. "Be careful, okay?"

Brad put both his hands on my shoulders. "You,

too. If Jenkins finds out we've been snooping around his place…" He didn't need to say anything more. If we were discovered, our lives would be forfeited, same as his father and Appleton.

"Wait!" Shar's voice rose outside. "Is the car fixed?"

"I saw something," the guard said. "Just hold on. I also know where Jenkins stashes a bottle of whiskey. I'll bring it out. We can have some fun."

Brad and I scrambled for a hiding place, squeezing under the desk and clicking off our lights. While being this close to the man was nice, my heart raced for another reason…the fear of discovery.

"Wait a minute. Why was the door unlocked?" The man muttered. "I must have forgotten to lock it when I did my earlier check. Won't make that mistake again."

The squeal of a metal drawer opening sounded loud in the trailer. A few seconds later, footsteps signaled the man leaving. Too bad for him, Brad and I would leave the door unlocked.

Hands gripped together, we peered out the window. Once the man was again focused on Shar, we exited the trailer and made a mad dash for the juniper bushes.

"I don't drink. Thanks for your help." Shar slammed the hood of the Thunderbird down, slid back into her car and sped away, leaving the poor guard standing there holding a half-empty whiskey bottle.

We congregated outside the penthouse. "We didn't find out anything," I said.

"I did." Shar grinned. "Leroy was full of information. He's out of town with the missus but returns in the morning. She'll be staying behind a few days. I hinted around about shady business deals, and he told me that Jenkins was also being investigated by the IRS. The man has more trouble coming than Santa has houses to visit on Christmas Eve."

"Well done." Brad smiled. "That gives me plenty to hint around about when I see him tomorrow."

"What are we going to be doing, Trinity?" Shar asked.

"Working as usual. Jenkins will get suspicious if we're all there. Brad will handle things and let us know what he finds out. Hopefully, it will be enough for McIlroy to make the arrest."

"Oh, the man will be arrested all right," Brad said. "I doubt I'll have much time to ask questions. He won't be charged with murder, though, and that's what I want."

"What time are you meeting him?"

"Six a.m." He glanced at the Rolex on his wrist. "Which means it's going to be a short night." He crooked his arm.

I slipped my hand in and strolled to the elevator after letting Shar know she could come in late in the morning if she needed to. Despite my tiredness, I plopped on the sofa and gathered by three cats into my lap while scratching behind Sheba's ears with my other hand. "Oh, my gosh. I'm not used to having a dog. She must need to go outside something awful."

"No worries there. I pay one of the maids to come take the dog out every couple of hours during the day."

I smiled up at him. "You really are the best. I can't believe I couldn't stand you at first."

His brows rose. "You couldn't stand me?"

I shrugged. "You were going to disrupt my life." And not in the good way he'd ended up changing it. "Since the dog has been cared for, I can take these three to bed with me. Goodnight, Brad."

"Goodnight. I'm glad you like me now." His words followed me to my room, sending heat to my face.

If he only knew how *much* I liked him.

Chapter 23

I headed into Tail-Waggin' the next morning with two pet carriers. There was no way I would leave the cats at home for one more day. I enjoyed having them at the store with me.

Brad's maid begged me to leave Sheba, so I did. Unfortunately, despite the fact she'd fallen in love with the massive dog, she couldn't keep her. Which meant, I was now the proud human of three cats and a big dog.

With a glance toward the theater, I caught sight of the Mercedes but not Brad or Jenkins. I let the cats out of the carriers and booted up my laptop, setting my cell phone close by. It wasn't opening time yet, so I wasn't officially late to work, but I was running later than usual for me.

"Good morning." Heather breezed into the store minus Robbie. "Thank you for finding Bobby."

"You're welcome. He was a great help in giving us a lead to Mr. Armstrong's killer." I smiled. "Where's the baby?"

"At daycare." She set her purse under the counter. "I qualify for state assistance now that Bobby and I are separated. Applied as soon as I kicked him out." Her lips turned down. "It's better this way, right?"

"Sure. Maybe you can work things out while he's in jail. Make a fresh start when he's released."

She nodded. "That would be nice." Pushing away from the desk, she turned the closed sign to open. "I'll sweep the sidewalk out front."

"Thanks." I returned my attention to emails, wishing I could do more to help my friend. After responding to a couple of requests for dog boarding, and someone who raised rabbits asking if I'd take the three she had left, I made a to-do list for the day. Priority one, order supplies. With business picking up, dog clothes and toys were flying off the shelves.

Sharkbait padded across my keyboard, signaling it was time he received some attention. "All right, big boy." I scratched the area right above his tail. "Why aren't you chasing Trashcan and Moses?" I fished a cat treat from a jar on the counter, making my cat happy. With a swish of his tail, he leaped to the floor allowing me to return to work.

"Sorry I'm late." Shar burst into the store. "I've five minutes before my first grooming appointment arrives. Can't believe I overslept."

"Understandable after last night." Oh no. Shar didn't close the door fast enough and I caught a glimpse of a furry orange tail as Moses dashed out and across the parking lot. "Hold down the fort," I yelled to Heather as I gave chase. Maybe next time, I should leave Moses home and only bring the other two.

The cat raced around the building and through a partially opened door at the back. I peered into the dark room. "Here kitty, kitty." Not receiving even a meow in response, I squeezed through the opening. Maybe I'd find the wayward cat purring in Brad's arms. They did seem to have formed an attachment.

I stood in a large expanse I assumed would one day be filled with theater seats and a large screen. The walls were being painted navy blue and burgundy stripes. The only light came from the glowing exit signs.

I headed for the theater entrance. The main part of the building lacked much progress. Piles of drywall and lumber, sawdust, and…white powder left over from cut drywall. Guess I knew where Moses spent the day he'd gone missing.

Where was Brad? His vehicle out front showed he was around. "Brad?" I shrieked as Moses raced from a dark corner and streaked past me.

"Come back here, you naughty kitty." My footsteps sounded loud on the concrete floor.

Moses darted up a set of stairs hidden behind a wall that I assumed would one day showcase upcoming movies. At the top was a closed door. Aha. Nowhere for Moses to go.

I grabbed the cat and held him close. He growled deep in his throat, his tail twitching in agitation. The hair on my arms rose to attention. Something was terribly wrong.

Keeping my gaze on the stairs, I reached behind me and turned the doorknob. Once it opened, I slipped inside. A window in one wall overlooked the atrium of the theater. Still holding tight to the squirming cat, I stared down.

Brad strode across the floor. Had he heard me call his name?

Harold Jenkins stepped from an alcove, a board raised high in his hands.

I slapped the glass. "Brad! Behind you!"

He glanced up, and then whirled. Instead of the board hitting his head, it slammed against the arm he raised in self-defense. I had to help him.

Glancing around the room for a weapon, and finding nothing except Moses, I dashed down the stairs. The room was empty. Where had Brad and Jenkins gone?

I spun, trying to see which way they'd gone. Drag marks in floor's dust showed someone had dragged someone toward the back. Please, God, don't let Brad be dead.

A breeze alerted me to a door open somewhere. I sniffed, detecting a faint scent of Infamous. Moses growled louder and fought harder for me to release him. When his hind claws raked my arm, I dropped him.

Feeling more alone than I'd ever felt in my life, I followed the drag marks into the dark recesses of the theater in search of the open door. I sniffed the air, trying to catch another whiff of Infamous. Since only Brad, Jenkins, myself, and Moses were in the building, it was safe to assume that Jenkins had killed Mr. Armstrong.

I patted my pocket for my cell phone before realizing I'd left it at the store. I almost headed back, but stopped. Brad might be seriously injured and need my help, so I couldn't spare a minute heading across the parking lot.

Doing my best to remain as quiet as possible so as not to alert Jenkins to my presence, I inched forward. A door slammed. I froze. Which way now? The further I went, the dimmer the room became.

Bad things happened in the dark. People got stabbed in the shower. My heart raced, and it took every ounce of courage I could muster to keep going. I focused on Brad, straining my ears for any sound.

The Infamous scent grew stronger. A footfall scuffed behind me. I whirled.

Jenkins held a gun aimed at my head. "You're a very nosy woman, Miss Ashford."

"Where's Brad?"

"You'll see him soon enough. Turn around and keep going in the direction you were." He gave the gun a jerk down the long dark hallway.

As I walked, I tried to come up with an escape plan. Without knowing my way around the theater, my options were slim.

"Turn right at the next auditorium," Jenkins said.

I entered another partially finished theater room. Holding a flashlight on a bound and gagged Brad stood Amber. My fingers curled, wanting to wrap themselves around her neck.

"Have a seat next to your boyfriend." Her smile chilled my blood.

"Which one of you killed Mr. Armstrong?" I sat next to Brad, relieved to see his eyes open.

"That would be me." Jenkins pulled up a metal

crate and sat across from us. "I also killed Appleton. The fact that I have to add two more deaths to my resume is your fault. Now, where are the blueprints?"

"The police have them."

He blinked a few times. "You found Langley?"

"Of course."

"Pretty proud of yourself, aren't you? Where's Mr. Armstrong's computer files?"

"I don't know." I fought not to glance at Brad. I really didn't know where the thumb drive was at that moment. Since I'm sure Jenkins searched Brad, I could be relatively sure the drive wasn't anywhere close.

"Since neither of you have what I want, I might as well kill you now."

"Then you'll never find them." I shrugged.

"Okay. Which should I do away with? You choose."

"Why is Amber with you? Isn't she Evans' mistress?"

"A girl can't have all her options in one place, Trinity." Amber rolled her eyes.

"You stabbed Summer."

"Her work was done."

Something clattered behind Jenkins.

He whirled and fired.

Moses howled. If I made it out of here alive, I'd make sure that cat got the best dish of food he'd ever had.

Scrambling to my feet, I tackled Jenkins around the knees and Brad kicked out at Amber.

The other man's gun slid across the floor,

disappearing into a dark corner.

I might not be big, but I could be ferocious when I need to be and latched onto Jenkins' back like a leech, leaving Brad, who'd slipped free of the twine around his wrists, to take care of Amber.

"Get off me!" Jenkins reached back and grabbed my ponytail.

"Not a chance." I tightened my arms around his neck and my legs around his waist, unsure how long I could hold on. Maybe more gym visits were in my future since I was quickly tiring.

Moses growled and swiped his claws at the man, ripping through the fabric of Jenkins' pants before the cat sprinted from the room.

"That cat hates you. He's a witness to Mr. Armstrong's murder, you know."

Jenkins hurled us backward into a wall. The breath whooshed from my body, and I lost my grip, sliding to the floor.

"Hold it right there." McIlroy and another officer rushed into the room. "Hands up, Jenkins. You, too, Miss Stirling."

Now that the cavalry had arrived, I rushed to Brad's side. "Are you hurt?"

"Think my arm's broken, especially after wrestling Amber." He caressed my face with his right hand. "What are you doing here?"

"Chasing after Moses." I smiled and leaned into his touch. "I told you that cat would find your father's killer."

He chuckled. "I have something for McIlroy. Come to the hospital with me?"

"I wouldn't dream of doing anything else."

Brad pulled his cell phone from his pocket. "Here's your recorded proof. I recorded both of their confessions on my phone. Now, if you'll excuse me, I need an x-ray."

"Good work, you two." McIlroy took the phone. "I'll need statements when you're up to it."

Brad put his good arm around my shoulders and steered me toward the door. "Will do."

Outside, he tossed me his car keys. "Mind driving?"

"Not at all. I do need to let Heather and Shar know I won't be back for a few hours."

"I'll wait here." He opened the car door and slid into the passenger seat.

I sprinted across the parking lot, told the others a short version of what had happened, asked that one of them find Moses, then left them with wide eyes as I returned to Brad. What a day, and it was barely noon. I slid into the driver's seat. "I can't believe I'm driving this."

Brad laughed. "If you're going to be my girl, then you might as well get used to nice things. I plan on spoiling you rotten."

"Am I your girl?" I turned in the seat.

"I'm hoping you will be. We make a good team, Trinity, but now that the adrenaline over almost being killed is wearing off, my arm is screaming."

"Oh, right." I grinned and started the car. If Mercedes had wings, I'd have flown us to the hospital on sheer joy. Brad wanted to be in a relationship with me. I couldn't imagine anything I'd like more.

"Do we have to be part of the country club?"

"Not unless you want to." He leaned his head against the seat and closed his eyes.

"Good. I can't stand the people who frequent that place."

"You were just unlucky enough to meet the bad ones." His lips curled. "It really is a nice place and has its perks. People will cater to your every need now."

That sounded tempting, but my needs were simple. "I'll think about it. For now, I want to go back to small-town country living where I didn't even know about that highfalutin-type of life."

Laughter burst from him. "I have a favor."

"Anything."

"I'd like to keep Moses, if you don't mind. The cat meant something to my father, and he did help save us back there by causing a distraction. Do you mind?"

"No. He belongs with you." Just as I did.

"Will you stay in the penthouse with me?"

I shook my head. "No. While it's nice and all, I like living close to my store." I cut him a sideways glance. "Plus, I'm an old-fashioned girl."

"Don't trust yourself around me?" He opened his eyes and winked.

Laughing, I pulled into the hospital parking lot. "That must be it." I exited the car and rounded it to help him out.

Brad cupped my face. "I'm going to kiss you, Trinity. I hope that's okay." His head lowered without waiting for my answer.

Who was I kidding? I lifted my face, closed my eyes, and let his lips take me to heaven.

The End

Check out the next book, The Dog Who Found a Body. Just aim your cell phone using a QR reader app on the QR code.

Website at www.cynthiahickey.com

Multi-published and Amazon and ECPA Best-Selling
author Cynthia Hickey has sold close to a million copies
of her works since 2013. She has taught a Continuing
Education class at the 2015 American Christian Fiction
Writers conference, several small ACFW chapters and
RWA chapters, and small writer retreats. She and her
husband run the small press, Winged Publications,
which includes some of the CBA's best well-known
authors. She lives in Arizona and Arkansas, becoming a
snowbird, with her husband and one dog. She has ten
grandchildren who keep her busy and tell everyone they
know that "Nana is a writer".

Connect with me on FaceBook
Twitter
Sign up for my newsletter and receive a free
short story
www.cynthiahickey.com

Follow me on Amazon
And Bookbub
Enjoy other books by Cynthia Hickey

Cozy Mysteries

Tiny House Mysteries
No Small Caper
Caper Goes Missing
Caper Finds a Clue
Caper's Dark Adventure
A Strange Game for Caper

Caper Steals Christmas
Caper Finds a Treasure

A Hollywood Murder
Killer Pose, book 1
Killer Snapshot, book 2
Shoot to Kill, book 3
Kodak Kill Shot, book 4
To Snap a Killer
Hollywood Murder Mysteries

Shady Acres Mysteries
Beware the Orchids, book 1
Path to Nowhere
Poison Foliage
Poinsettia Madness
Deadly Greenhouse Gases
Vine Entrapment

Nosy Neighbor Series
Anything For A Mystery, Book 1
A Killer Plot, Book 2
Skin Care Can Be Murder, Book 3
Death By Baking, Book 4
Jogging Is Bad For Your Health, Book 5
Poison Bubbles, Book 6
A Good Party Can Kill You, Book 7 (Final)
Nosy Neighbor collection

Christmas with Stormi Nelson

The Summer Meadows Series
Fudge-Laced Felonies, Book 1
Candy-Coated Secrets, Book 2
Chocolate-Covered Crime, Book 3
Maui Macadamia Madness, Book 4

All four novels in one collection

The River Valley Mystery Series
Deadly Neighbors, Book 1
Advance Notice, Book 2
The Librarian's Last Chapter, Book 3
All three novels in one collection

Brothers Steele
Sharp as Steele
Carved in Steele
Forged in Steele
Brothers Steele (All three in one)

The Brothers of Copper Pass
Wyatt's Warrant
Dirk's Defense
Stetson's Secret
Houston's Hope
Dallas's Dare
Seth's Sacrifice
Malcolm's Misunderstanding

Fantasy
Fate of the Faes
Shayna
Deema
Kasdeya

Time Travel
The Portal

Wife for Hire – Private Investigators
Saving Sarah
Lesson for Lacey
Mission for Meghan

CYNTHIA HICKEY

Long Way for Lainie
Aimed at Amy
Wife for Hire (all five in one)

CLEAN BUT GRITTY Romantic Suspense

Highland Springs

Murder Live
Say Bye to Mommy
To Breathe Again
Highland Springs Murders (all 3 in one)

Colors of Evil Series

Shades of Crimson
Coral Shadows

The Pretty Must Die Series

Ripped in Red, book 1
Pierced in Pink, book 2
Wounded in White, book 3
Worthy, The Complete Story

Lisa Paxton Mystery Series

Eenie Meenie Miny Mo
Jack Be Nimble
Hickory Dickory Dock

Secrets of Misty Hollow

Hearts of Courage
A Heart of Valor
The Game
Suspicious Minds
After the Storm
Local Betrayal

Overcoming Evil series
Mistaken Assassin
Captured Innocence
Mountain of Fear
Exposure at Sea
A Secret to Die for
Collision Course
Romantic Suspense of 5 books in 1

INSPIRATIONAL

Historical cozy
Hazel's Quest

Historical Romances
Runaway Sue
Taming the Sheriff
Sweet Apple Blossom
A Doctor's Agreement
A Lady Maid's Honor
A Touch of Sugar
Love Over Par
Heart of the Emerald
A Sketch of Gold
Her Lonely Heart

Finding Love the Harvey Girl Way
Cooking With Love
Guiding With Love
Serving With Love
Warring With Love
All 4 in 1

A Wild Horse Pass Novel
They Call Her Mrs. Sheriff, book 1 (A Western
Romance)

Finding Love in Disaster
The Rancher's Dilemma
The Teacher's Rescue
The Soldier's Redemption

Woman of courage Series

A Love For Delicious
Ruth's Redemption
Charity's Gold Rush
Mountain Redemption
Woman of Courage series (all four books)

Short Story Westerns
Desert Rose
Desert Lilly
Desert Belle
Desert Daisy
Flowers of the Desert 4 in 1

Contemporary

Romance in Paradise
Maui Magic
Sunset Kisses

Deep Sea Love
3 in 1

Finding a Way Home
Service of Love
Hillbilly Cinderella
Unraveling Love
I'd Rather Kiss My Horse

Christmas
Dear Jillian
Romancing the Fabulous Cooper Brothers
Handcarved Christmas
The Payback Bride
Curtain Calls and Christmas Wishes
Christmas Gold
A Christmas Stamp
Snowflake Kisses
Merry's Secret Santa
A Christmas Deception

The Red Hat's Club (Contemporary novellas)

Finally
Suddenly
Surprisingly
The Red Hat's Club 3 – in 1

Short Story

One Hour (A short story thriller)
Whisper Sweet Nothings (a Valentine short romance)

Made in United States
North Haven, CT
27 March 2024

50583528R00117